Elton T. Brown

A History of the Great Minnesota Forest Fires

Sandstone, Mission Creek, Hinckley, Pokegama, Skunk Lake

Elton T. Brown

A History of the Great Minnesota Forest Fires
Sandstone, Mission Creek, Hinckley, Pokegama, Skunk Lake

ISBN/EAN: 9783337255299

Printed in Europe, USA, Canada, Australia, Japan

Cover: Foto ©Andreas Hilbeck / pixelio.de

More available books at **www.hansebooks.com**

A HISTORY

OF THE

GREAT MINNESOTA

FOREST FIRES,

Sandstone,   Mission Creek,

Hinckley,

Pokegama,   Skunk Lake.

. . BY . .

ELTON T. BROWN.

ORIGINAL ILLUSTRATIONS.

BY

CARL C. BROWN.

BROWN BROS. PUBLISHERS.

ST. PAUL,   MINN.

A TRIBUTE.

By the Author.

Gone from the haunts, where they loved and they lingered,
Gone from the paths that their feet loved to roam,
Bereft are the friends that revered and that mingled
Daily with those whom the fire has called home.

Men stricken down in the bloom of their man-hood,
Women, whose hearts were proved true as steel,
Children, whose eyes had brought light to the household,
Suffered and died, still mute with appeal.

There were heroes, whose story will ne'er be related,
There were heroines too, who will e'er be unsung,
Self-sacrifice truly, of all attribute noble,
Thy name from the top of the peak should be flung.

They are gone, leaving naught but the ashes behind them,
They are gone, yet we can but rejoice at their gain,
Their trials are all over, no ill can betide them;
While we must work on, till we meet them again.

. . . PREFACE . . .

IN launching this little volume upon the turbulent sea of an existence which may or may not prove altogether satisfactory, the author feels called upon to state that in this work it is not his aim or desire to make an especially interesting and readable volume, but more particularly to chronicle a few facts in as terse a manner as may be relative to, he thinks without exception, the most horrible calamity which has befallen any portion of the human race in modern times. He desires that what facts he here presents may be absolutely authentic in every detail, and his purpose in giving this work to the public is to place in a concise and readable form a full account of the fire in its awful voracity together with a description of the country over which it passed, and enough personal experiences to give the reader some small idea of the excruciating suffering of the survivors. Also the efforts of a generous people to alleviate their suffering, as well as the heroic efforts of those upon whose courage and strength of character rested the lives of many hundred human beings. Pen cannot picture and tongue cannot tell the whole story. Young men will grow gray and their children gray and still history will hold no parallel to the Hinckley Forest Fires. The Johnstown Tragedy, so-called pales into insignificance beside it, as to the area affected and the amount of property destroyed, if not as to loss of life; and let us hope and pray that from this time on we may be delivered from so terrible an ordeal as has just been undergone by the good people of Kanabec, Pine and Aitkin Counties in Minnesota and Douglas, Burnett and adjoining Counties in Wisconsin.

CONTENTS.

APPENDIX.

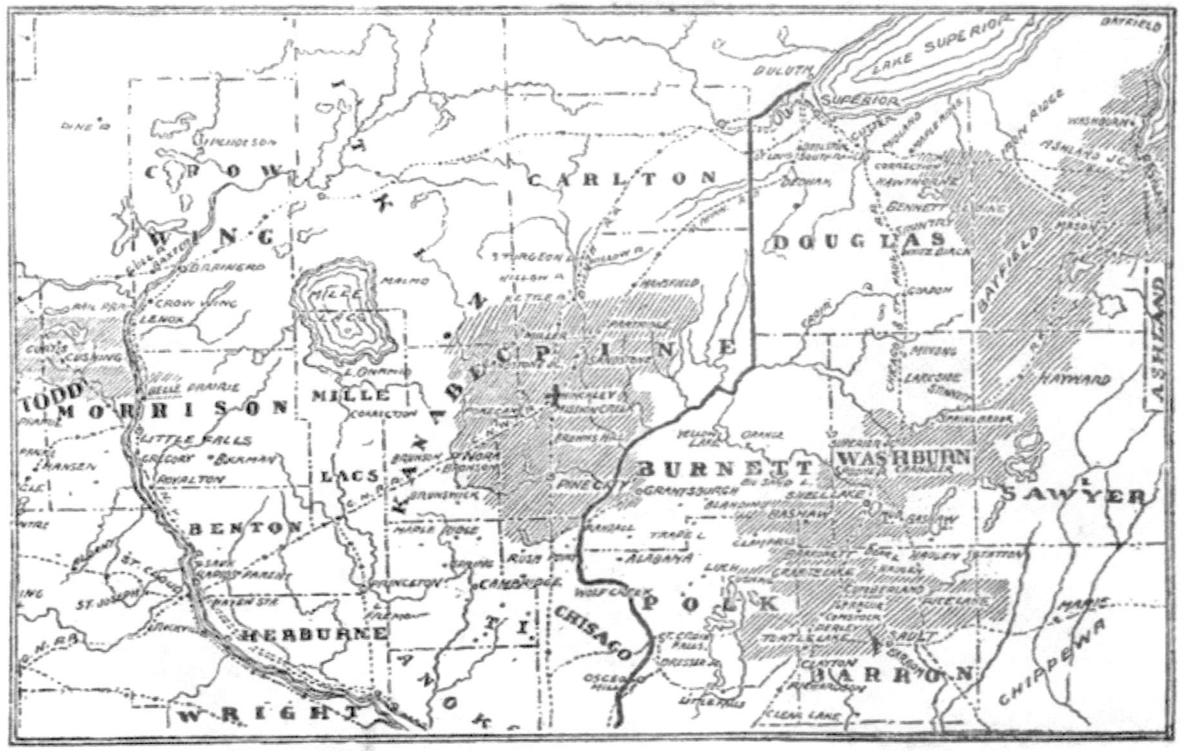

THE FIRE DISTRICT

THE HISTORY

OF THE

GREAT MINNESOTA FOREST FIRES.

CHAPTER I.

THE SURROUNDING COUNTRY.

EVEN the most casual observer in passing through on the line of the St. Paul & Duluth Ry. between St. Paul and Duluth could not fail to be impressed with almost a sense of wonder at the magnitude and extent of the lumber interests in the adjoining country. Lumber on all sides; every station had its mill and every farmhouse its rods of piled cord-wood, posts or piling as the case might be or as the industrious owner might see fit to get out. Gigantic pines rose straight as an arrow from 100 to 150 feet in the air, standing side by side, so close that the clump of branches at their tops inter-locked one with the other, making a canopy so dense and so complete that the sun was dismayed in its attempt to pierce its shadows and its noon-day brightness only lightened the shade to a dusky twilight. As far as the eye could reach on all sides were forests, or the stumpage where they had been cleared away and in lieu of them had grown little homes and farm-houses of more portentious proportions, nestled in among the pines like islands in an inland sea, where some voyager more venturous than the rest had plighted his faith and built his cot with the hope and prayer that the land he toiled to clear might yield at least a living if not a livelihood. And for the most part, fortune seemed to smile on these dwellers in the pines. Mills had sprung up, railroads come in, wages had been good and work plenty all the year round. Lumber was a staple product and here was an almost inexhaustible expanse of the finest timber only waiting the axe and the saw to convert it into money or its equivalent. Is it any wonder that the great lumber companies looked upon this section as the reservoir of their existence, and that they appreciated its value and were not slow in profiting by it?

Thousands of men were gathered from our Northwestern cities every year and sent to work in the woods in this section for the winter, and millions of feet of logs were banked ready for the drive every spring. Hundreds of men were employed in the saw-mills converting these logs into lumber all through the summer season, so that the Pine county agriculturalist was given the very best of markets, i. e. the home market, for everything he could raise and was paid a good price for it, too.

The dairy interests of the section were of no small importance. The underbrush in the woods made excellent pasturage and a large proportion of the Duluth and Superior milk supply was gathered from this section. A special milk train so-called being run into these sections on the Duluth road every morning, and aside from the milk much of the butter and other dairy products for the supply of the Duluth markets came from this region. As is the case with most of our rural districts, the people of this section were made up of a heterogeneous mass of humanity gathered together from the four corners of the Earth. Former residents of the Scandinavian Peninsular were perhaps in the majority with a goodly sprinkling of the subjects of the German Emperor, whose thrifty neat looking log cabins stood out in sharp contrast to the more dilapidated habitations of their less industrious neighbors. Aside from the lumber camps were the farmers who ranged from the poor squatter with an acre or two of potatoes which he had planted between the stumps, his sturdy wife and abundant family, his cow, his pig and his shack, to the farmer who would tell you he came here in the fall of '68 and who by dint of hard work and watching the pennies had built a very pleasant little home about him, and was preparing to spend his old age with comparative ease and comfort.

And so they dwell secure in their houses fearing nothing, never dreaming that so awful a calamity as befell them was possible, or that they stood in any danger whatever from the source which was destined to wreak such havoc and spread such dire desolation in the lap of prosperity and plenty. Forest fires had been frequent and terrible, it is true, considerable damage to young trees especially had been done every fall by forest fires, but they had for the most part been easily checked and no one apprehended that the season of '94 would differ in this respect from that of '93 or any of the other years. All expected forest fires, they always came to a greater or less extent every fall as some indolent vagrant would drop a match in the tinder of a bed of pine needless, or some stumpage which had been brushed, grubbed and burned over had gotten unmanageable and left a blackened and bleak track in the wake of its demon; or again a spark from a passing locomotive would fall where a breath of wind would fan it into life and it would grow till perhaps a mile or two of pines had been devoured by its incipient onslaught. Up to this time there had been no loss of life from this source and comparatively little loss of property. The usual precautions had been taken to prevent the spread of fires should they occur and especial care had been given to guarding against the starting of new ones, as the populace as a whole appreciated the fact that the dryness of the earlier part of the season would make a forest fire especially dangerous at this time. It was perhaps, more owing to the fact that the residents as a whole apprehended no danger, that the death list reached such appalling proportions. Many who might have escaped had they made the attempt at the time of the first alarm felt that the towns were at least safe until it was too late for them to rectify their mistake and they were overtaken by a death too horrible to contemplate. No one can view a forest fire without feeling impressed with its awful and almost majestically terrible advance, not slowly not carefully, as if the demon was inclined to torture his victims with any degree of suspense, but with a sweep and a surge that was something terrible to contemplate even in its mildest form. Mounting a gigantic pine almost as a flash of powder in the pan, carrying the burning cinders high into the air, dropping them far over and beyond, where they would slowly descend in circles of light into branches of another pine, only to repeat the operation again and again, carrying the fire forward with almost incredible rapidity, until it reached a clearing or had burned itself out. As to most of my readers, the various towns mentioned in the text will be known only on paper, it may not be out of place to give in a few words a brief outline of the location of the different towns and the industries upon which for the most part each was to a great extent dependent.

Hinckley was perhaps the largest and most important point in the fire swept district. It was here that a number of the most heroic episodes of the fire took place and where by far the greatest number of people perished in the flames. It was a thriving town on the St. Paul & Duluth R. R. seventy-seven miles North-east from St. Paul. It was practically built and maintained by the Brennan Lumber Co. which concern owned a large lumber plant at Hinckley and which employed from 300 to 400 men the year round. Its lumber mills were fed by logs which were floated down the North and South branches of the Grindstone River which flow southeasterly and joined within the limits of the town. Hinckley is also the junction of the Great Northern and St. Paul & Duluth Ry's.

Mission Creek is a small station three miles south of Hinckley on the St. Paul & Duluth R. R. The John Martin Lumber Co. had mills at this point.

Pokegama is a small station on the Eastern Minnesota R. R. eight miles southwest of Hinckley on Pokegama Creek.

Wareham is a small station on the Great Northern R. R. sixty-three miles South-west from Duluth and seven miles North-west of Hinckley.

Sandstone, next to Hinckley was perhaps the most important point in the afflicted section, and was the scene of terrible loss of life. It is a thriving town on the Eastern Minnesota Ry., nine miles from Hinckley on the Kettle River. Its principal support were the Sandstone quarries In the bluffs by the river, and it was from these quarries that its name is derived. The scenery at Sandstone presents much that is picturesque and grand.

Miller and Finlayson are small stations on the St. Paul & Duluth R. R. between Hinckley and Kettle River.

Kettle River or Rutledge is on the line of the St. Paul & Duluth R. R. sixteen miles from Hinckley.

Partridge, a station on the Eastern Minnesota R. R. sixteen miles from Hinckley; of no great commercial importance but in the scene of the conflagration.

Pine City, was the nearest point to the fire swept district which was unharmed and from this point the relief committees did their noble work. It is on the line of the St. Paul & Duluth R. R., sixty-four miles from St. Paul and ninety-one from Duluth. The Snake River which flows through the town practically forms the Southern Boundary of the havoc wrought by the fire fiend. The name of Pine City will be long remembered as one which was intimately connected with the Hinckley calamity. It has one or two steam saw mills and is a thriving community of about six hundred people.

Cumberland, on Beaver Dam Lake on the Chicago, St. Paul, Minneapolis & Omaha road in Wisconsin in Barron County, is a live town with a population of about one thousand people, in the limits of the fire swept country; it was not injured to any great extent but was a point that the relief committee made a basis of operation.

Barronett, a village with a population of about five hundred people in Barron County, on the Omaha road seven and a half miles Northeast from Cumberland. The village was built and practically maintained by the Barronett Lumber Co., which operated a large mill at the place, kept a general store and gave employment to nearly all the people of the town. Barronett was completely destroyed not a vestige of it remaining.

Bashaw was a post office in Burnett County ten and a half miles from Shell Lake the nearest railroad station. Bashaw's total population did not exceed sixty people and it suffered terribly from the fire fiend.

Rice Lake, an incorporated town of twenty-five hundred people, on the Omaha road about ten miles east of Cumberland. It was not injured to any extent by fire but was a point of distribution for the relief.

Granite Lake is a station on the Omaha road about four miles south of Barronett. Of small importance but was totally consumed.

Cable and Drummond were small towns on the Omaha road in Bayfield Co. The centre of a sparsely settled district which was burned over and which was damaged to a greater or less extent by the fire.

Ashland, Wis., an important City on the south shore Chequamegon Bay, an inlet of Lake Superior, quite a railroad centre and a metropolis of the whole section known as Northern Wisconsin, three-hundred and forty.four miles from Milwaukee and one hundred and eighty-four miles from St. Paul. During the summer months while the lake is open Ashland holds quite an important position as a lake port, immense quantities of lumber, ore and grain are shipped annually east over the lake route from this place. A number of fine saw-mills and planing mills are in operation here, and altogether it is a very lively, wide-awake berg. Population, from twelve to fifteen-thousand people.

Washburn, the terminal of the Omaha road is situated on the north shore of Chequamegon Bay, directly across the bay from Ashland. It is a place of no small commercial importance both as a railroad centre, a lumbering point and a lake port.

It contains quite a number of large lumbering plants and lumber mills, and is a natural outlet for an immense tract of timber land which was swept by the great fire. Washburn itself had a very narrow escape.

CHAPTER II.

THE FIRE.

SEPTEM-
BER first
1 8 9 4 ,
m a r k s
an epoch
in the an-
nals of
Minne-
sota,
which will long be remembered as one of the most
horrible, history has to relate. Day dawned at
Hinckley much as other days had done many times
in its existence, with a hazy blue smoke enveloping
everything, softening the rough harsh lines of the
landscape and giving instead a mellow glow of sunlight that was both pleasant and beautiful to look
upon. Forest fires had been raging to the South
of them for some time. For nearly three months
at one place or another the fire would start and
run over a mile or two of woodland and either die

down or smolder until another opportunity or a-
nother breeze swept it in another direction and
gave it a new lease of life. All noticed that the
smoke had grown more troublesome than on the
the preceeding day. They knew the fire had come
closer to the town but not one had ever dreamed
that ere nightfall their pleasant little berg would
be literally wiped out of existance, and that over
two hundred of its people would have passed to
the realm beyond.

They were sturdy, hardy fellows these men of the
Northern Pines and they felt that in case of peril
they could cope with any ordinary blaze. They
had a thoroughly organized Fire-Brigade, with a
good equipment and paraphernalia necessary for
the work. Then is it any wonder they were loth to
leave? No such calamity had ever been known, they
had no precedent of this sort and it is only natural
for one to feel secure in his own door-yard.

They, perhaps, did not fully appreciate the condition which made this different from other days.
In the first place, the entire section could be well
compared to a gigantic tinder-box, waiting only
the spark to burst into a huge sheet of flame. The
season had been almost entirely lacking of moisture,
no rain having fallen for nearly three months, or
since the early part of June; the corn drooped, the
potatoes withered, and on all sides could be heard
the cry for rain; even the maples and other deciduous

After the fire had passed.

Hinckley before the fire.

trees shriveled and wilted, and the ground itself lay open in great cracks as the parched earth endeavored to draw a little moisture from the heated atmosphere. The dust laid thick on the field and in the roads following the passers-by in great clouds and making the very life of the traveler miserable.

Just where the fire originated and when, will probably never be known. Half a dozen different fires were known to have been burning in the section swept by the great fire, and which one acted as the match to the magazine is of course hard to determine.

It may be altogether fanciful and it may not, but the writer has heard the following theory of the origin of the Hinckley blaze and will put it in writing with the admonition that it be taken for what it is worth. As has already been stated fires had been raging in one district or another adjacent to Hinckley for nearly three months prior to the memorable first day of September. The air was thoroughly saturated with smoke and had been for days, so much so that the horizon presented that peculiar atmospheric phenomena which we usually witness during our Indian summer when everything takes on a hazy indistinctness and the light blue of the earth mingles with the deep blue of the sky and it is hard to determine where the one begins and the other ends. It is a demonstrated fact that large quantities of fine dust floating in an

atmosphere which is entirely free from moisture,
as was true in this case, will in the course of time
ignite from spontaneous combustion, and it is a
theory held out by some that the charcoal dust
and carbon which had been absorbed by the atmosphere in this section, became so heated by the long
continued drought that spontaneous combustion
was produced and culminated in this terrible calamity. Nor are the proofs entirely lacking that
would tend to prove that this version of the story
is not all moonshine. Those who witnessed it say
that the air itself seemed to be on fire and the
manner in which the fire advanced would tend to
prove this theory. It did not, as is usually the case,
burn along from bush to bush, or from tree to
tree, but seemed to make great leaps, oftimes breaking out fifteen hundred or two thousand feet ahead
of the foremost blaze without any apparent cause,
or any means of communication but the air itself.
One man who took refuge in a lake at least fifteen
hundred feet in width tells of actually seeing great
balls of fire leap from the burning forest on one
side to the unscathed pines on the other, there to
renew the dire desolation which it had already
spread in its track. Another, a farmer who by
dint of hard work had succeeded in clearing some
fifteen acres of ground and had built a little home
upon it, said that he had prepared to fight the fire
on earth, but was not fortified against a fire from

the heavens, saying that it literally rained fire for some minutes before they were struck by the wave of heat which presaged the fiery hurricane and which proved so disastrous to so many human beings.

A very significent fact in this connection, and one that is rather difficult to account for is that the houses on the south side of the town proper at Hinckley, which, from the direction of the wind one would naturally suppose would be the first to go, were as a matter of fact the last structures in the town to catch fire.

All the survivors of the calamity speak of having noticed in its outset the same peculiar phenomena. The wind was terrific and the smoke so black and dense that it was impossible to see anything three feet away. The air was thoroughly impregnated with carbon and heavily charged with gas, suddenly there was a report, and the whole mass of smoke burst into a living sheet of flame with a roar which was that of thunder and that was followed by a crackling and burning of everything inflamble of all descriptions within the scope of the blaze.

That fires of this description have been known to occur in this section is vouched for by the following extract from a letter to the writer from a prominent attorney of the city of Duluth:

"It was in June, 1872, after a rainless spring that fires started in the woods of Northern Wisconsin, were feeding on the pine and fir forests to the south of us, and gradually working toward the lake."

"Upon a certain day, shortly after sunrise, the wall of smoke hanging over the forests toward the south, was suddenly bent in our direction by a gale from that quarter. So sudden was this movement that we, who had estimated the fire to be at least fifteen miles distant, were surprised a few moments later to see the tree tops across the bay some three miles distant, all ablaze. No smoke was then visible. It soon, however, began again to roll up and was carried by the strong wind like a great black monster across the river (here about half a mile in width) enveloping Grassy Point in its folds and seeming to swallow up the tall pines of the forest, just west of the little village of Oneota. We were fortunate in being out of the track of the monster, else there would have been none left to tell the tale."

"The column of smoke had reached the valley and began to climb the mountain in less time than it takes to write this description. While we were standing in the clear sunlight gazing at the wall of smoke before us, a bolt of fire like a flash of lightning—shot from the Wisconsin shores through the black ribs of the monster, and seemed to ignite the whole mass in a moment. A subdued roar, a crackling, hissing sound, one moment a wall of the densest, blackest smoke, the next, a blood red flame, and next we could look through the woods and along Grassy Point, smokeless uow, but all ablaze, roaring and crackling towards the mountain."

"As before, the smoke began to roll up and hide the ravages of the flame. As the fire led to what is known as the gorge, a deep, rocky glen, back of Oneota, and as there was no immediate danger of the town being burned, unless the wind should suddenly change, a few of us young fellows repaired as rapidly as possible to a place near the glen and succeeded in gaining a point of vantage on the south-east side of the glen, in a little clearing on an elevated plateau, where we had a good view of the fire ,looking up the glen which was at that time,densely wooded with pine, fir, cedar etc. Before we had reached our stand, the smoke had rolled up the mountin and down the rocky sides of the glen, completely filling the gorge, and driven by the gale had passed to the northward. We had come to witness again the phenomena first mentioned. We had not long to wait, a blinding flash and the whole world before us seemed to be ablaze. In ten seconds or perhaps less, every particle of smoke was consumed and we could look down and through the glen, now all ablaze, which ten seconds before was green with verdure and growing trees."

"We stayed here for some time watching the smoke explosions which seemed afterwards confined to this glen and occured at intervals of about fifteen minutes, as if the dense woods burning within its rocky sides furnished the gases, which being somewhat confined by the bluffs on either side, were not swept along by the gale and accumulating here, were again and again ignited; now black as mid-night, now flaming red, and next as clear as ether. As we stood looking at these changes I noted particularly how clearly one could see down and through the glen, after the cloud of smoke was consumed and before it began to form again."

"I remember of having said to my companion, If Dante had seen a glen like this, at a time like this, he would have been able to describe a Hell, which would have put a fear of God into the hearts of his readers and no mistake."

"The impression I received on that June day, time can never efface. The dense columus of smoke now rolling majestically upwards, now toru and riven by the wind into fantastic forms and black as mid-night, now flaming red and in a moment gone, leaving in its place a vacuum as transparent as space, now deafening the ear with its roar; now still as death and again seething, crackling, hissing, sounding at one time like the roll of distant thunder, or the ocean surf trampling on the sea shore, and again lapsing into death-like silence."

Although the exact origin of the fire is somewhat indefinite the fact is very plain to even the most casual observer that the fire must have started in at least two or perhaps three different points almost similtaneously.

One of these points must have been in the region south of Mission Creek, in Minnesota, and the other about fifty miles east and twenty miles south of this place, at or near Cumberland or Rice Lake, in Wisconsin. While the eastern, or Barronette fire, if I may be pardoned for using this term, to distinguish it from the western, or Hinckley blaze, may have covered as much territory and been as terrible to endure as was the Hinckley horror, its possibilities for the destruction of life were not as large as lay in the path of the western demon. Hinckley itself probably held as many people at the outbreak of the calamity as all the towns affected by the eastern fires put together. As this is true, it is also a fact that the loss of life at Hinckley was much greater than in any other section of the burned district, so it behooves us in giving an authentic history to devote more space to the sufferings of the Hinckleyites than to any other section.

The first intimation to the people of Hinckley

that anything unusual was soon to occur was a-
bout noon, when the smoke, which had been rather
troublesome all the morning, seemed to grow more
dense and was accompanied by a heat which, though
it was not much, was enough to be quite percept-
able. No one thought anything of it or was a-
larmed about it until an hour later, when as it
still increased, they thought the Fire Department
might have something to do before the afternoon
was over, and an occasional group would be seen
wistfully watching the southern sky and joking a-
bout their ability as fire fighters. The storm cloud
itself, which, when it burst, swept everything before it, rose like an almost perpendicular wall of ·
black smoke surging and roaring and rolling, rising into the very heavens as far as the eye could
reach. It was hardly a time to contemplate the
sublime and majestic, but the sight of that terrible
cloud of fire in its irresistable onslaught was a
wonderful demonstration of the power of the elements and enough to make the strongest man
quake and beg for mercy in his very weakness and
insignificance. Some small idea of the awfulness
of this disaster can be gleaned from the fact that
the storm cloud's roar was heard at Pine City fifteen miles away, where it appeared to be only a
short distance off; they had no idea that it reached
Hinckley, or that Hinckley had been destroyed until the news was brought in by the survivors.

Although the wind had blown a gale from the south all the morning, about half-past one it seemed to gain strength and gradually increased until at about four o'clock when its fury was at its height, its velocity was at least sixty miles an hour. In certain sections of the forest over which the fire passed, where all evidence of the work of the wind has not been entirely obliterated, the trees are all up-rooted bodily by the wind and are found all lying in one direction, showing that the wind came directly from the south and was the direct wind of the hurricane rather than the twisting motion of the cyclone.

Another gruesome feature of the occasion and one that added much to the bewilderment and frightfulness of the scene was that during the period that the wind was at its height, owing to the combined influences of the cloud and the smoke from the ruins, it was as dark as mid-night, except when the fire reached some material more inflamable than the rest, it would flare up and light up the scene giving it an appearance very similar to a flash of lightning in a thunder storm.

Very few people, unless they have given the matter some little study and thought have any conception of the fire nor of the country which was traversed by its flames. While for the most part our descriptions so far have been confined to the country immediately adjacent to Hinckley the fire covered a region of over twenty-five hundred square miles of surface and extended over a strip of territory from twenty to fifty miles in width, and from one hundred to one hundred and twenty-five miles in length, comprising parts of Washburn, Sawyer, Douglas, Bayfield, Barron and Burnett Counties in Wisconsin, and Pine, Kenabec and Aitkin Counties in Minnesota.

We do not wish to be understood as stating that this entire section was burned over, but that portions of the fire covered this entire district. It seemed to burn in strips leaving a belt of timber untouched, while on both sides the flames had laid waste hundreds of acres of pine lands. All this section is of the same general character, that is, it abounds in pine lands and lumber interests.

The western portion was by far the most thickly settled of any part and it was in this section that the fury of the fire seemed to wreak its vengence on a helpless and unsuspecting community almost without warning. Farther east it was more like the ordinary forest fire, and was more as they expected and in some cases they were not only able to save themselves but their stock and occasionally their buildings.

A peculiar feature of this conflagration and without doubt the most horrible and excruciating part of the whole terrible affair was the wave of heat that is described by all the survivors, as accompanying the first fierce burst of the storm.

It was by the intense heat of this first wave that most of those who make up the death list came to their untimely end   As the condition of nearly all of the bodies after the fire had passed would indicate that the victims had died not from the flames themselves, but from the inhalation of the hot gases of this first wave. As for instance a man who evidently had been running, was found with his foot raised for another step, in which position he he had died as he was overtaken by the heat, and a number of similar cases could be cited which go to show that God was merciful and that death came in many cases instantly instead of by slow degrees of torture as would naturally be expected in a case of this kind. Mr. Fraser whose miraculous escape will be cronicled in the ensuing pages says that when the wave struck the one hundred and twenty people who lost their lives on the wagon road north of Hinckley, there was one piercing cry of mortal agony and then all was still, the literal stillness of death itself.

As this fire differed from others in its extent and in the velocity of the wind, in the same degree was its heat more intense and of much longer duration than the average forest fires.

It was the ordinary thing in a forest fire that the fire should run over the ground, burn the underbrush and fallen limbs, but it did as a rule comparitivly little damage to the trees for lumbering purposes. Oftimes the pines were killed or died from the effects of the fire, but it was seldom that they were actually burned. In this case however, while it does not hold true in all parts of the fire swept district, in certain portions of the western section the heat was so intense it not only burned the underbrush and the pines, roots, trunks and all but actually consumed the top earth, or loam, and where had been a forest of standing pine and underbrush there is nothing left but the clay subsoil and the rocks and stones which happened to be held in the upper deposit. Of course this is not true over the entire section but in certain portions where the fire was the hottest this condition of affairs exists, while in certain other portions which from some unknown cause had the benefit of a cool current of air, the appearance does not differ materially from other forest fires.

It was a very noticeable fact that the heat increased in the degree of its intensity with the number of miles which it had burned over, or in other words it was more intense at Hinckley than at Mission Creek and still more severe and destructive at Sandstone than at Hinckley or in any other part of the doomed section.

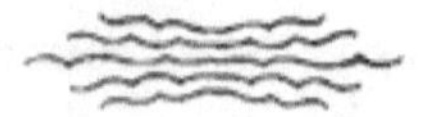

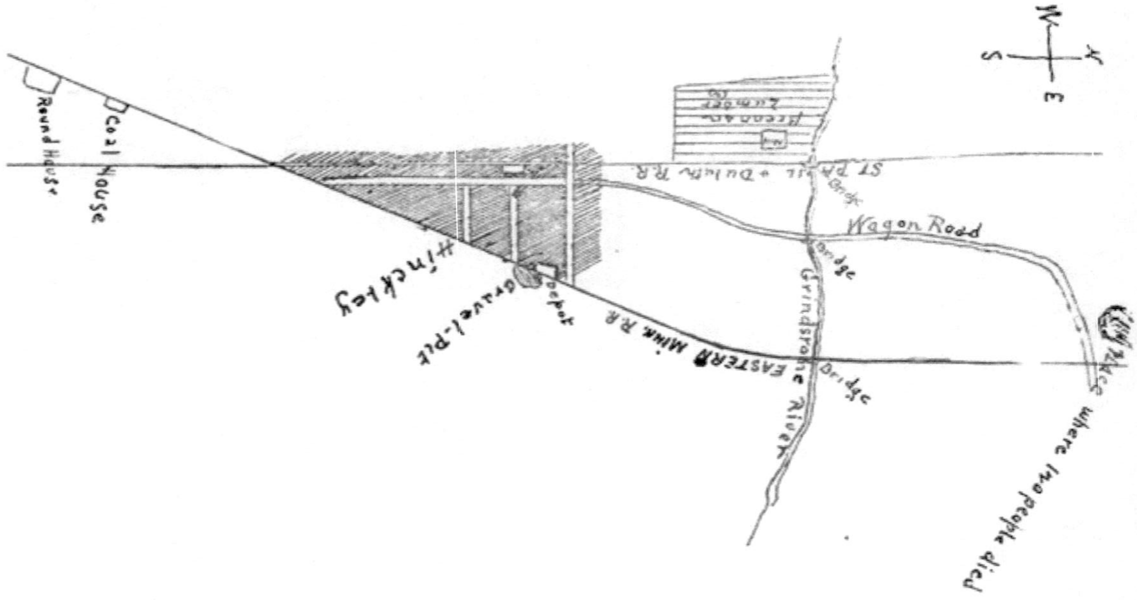

MAP OF HINCKLEY AND VICINITY

CHAPTER III

THE EMERGENCY TRAIN

glance at the accompanying cut of the plat of the town of Hinckley will give a better understanding of the events chronicled in the following pages than would otherwise be possible. Hinckley was an incorporated village of about twelve hundred inhabitants, situated at the junction of the St. Paul & Duluth and Eastern Minnesota Railways, which is a part of the G. N. system, seventy-seven miles from St. Paul and seventy miles from Duluth. Both roads run in a northerly direction and have Duluth for their destination. They crossed each other just south of the town proper.

The depots of the respective roads were situated

a short distance north of the junction and about
fifteen hundred feet apart. All of the business portion of Hinckley, and in fact all of the town with
the exception of a few buildings west of the Duluth
tracks lay between these two roads, while directly north of it about a quarter of a mile distant ran
the Grindstone River. This stream ran directly
east and west and was crossed by both railroads
and by a wagon-bridge which was situated about
midway between the railroad bridges.

Just east of the Eastern Minnesota track and in
fact directly east of the town itself is the gravel pit
which will be refered to later. It is about three
acres in extent and held from two to three feet of
water at the time of the fire. It was the nearest
and proved to be the safest possible means of escape
from the fury of the flames.

On the day of the fire the north bound Limited
from St. Paul to Duluth, on the St. Paul & Duluth road reached Hinckley at 2 o'clock, two hours
late, and a few of the more timorous and those
who felt the danger at that time escaped on that
train. The local freight on the Eastern Minnesota
which has a daily run from Duluth to Hinckley and
return reached Hinckley at 2:40. The south bound
passenger on the Eastern Minnesota was due at
Hinckley at 3:25 and arrived on time. The freight
waited until the arrival of the passenger, when the
two crews made up a combination train which was

one of the principal means of escape of the affright-
ed people.

The south bound Limited on the Duluth road,
from Duluth to St. Paul was due at Hinckley at
4:05. It ran within about a mile and a half of the
town, where it was met by the townspeople, and
learning the bridge was unsafe, ran back to Skunk
Lake, a little lake near the track about five and a
half miles from Hinckley, where its passengers
passed through a frightful, yet succesful battle for
their lives.

Penned in on three sides by a wall of fire, east,
west and south alike presenting a sea of flames, in
the agony of the hour their natural direction to
escape was toward the north, and following this
impulse, a number of citizens, nearly crazed with
fear followed the wagon road which leads out from
Hinckley to the north and as the following pages
will relate enacted the most heart rending act in
this awful drama. A few fled to the river but more
trusted their safety to the gravel pit. It was to
one or the other of these channels that the survivors
owe their lives to-day and the methods they took
to reach them and how it fared with them in their
respective stations as well as how the grim reaper
came to those of them who are now past the bourne
from which no traveler returns, it is the writer's
mission to relate.

About two o'clock in the afternoon the Fire Department of Hinckley was called to the west side of the town to fight a slight blaze which had broken out there and as the fire was seen to be approaching quite close to the town, it was feared it might get obstreperous so it was thought best to be on guard. Two thousand feet of hose was laid down and as that was found to be inadequate to reach the hottest blaze a telegram was sent to Rush City for six hundred feet more. That telegram however, was never answered, and the hose never arrived, as ere that was possible, Hinckley, as it had been, was a thing of the past.

It was about two o'clock that the department was first called out and ere half an hour had elapsed half a dozen small buildings in the outskirts were in flames. The wind was blowing a perfect hurricane from a direction a little west of south. The smoke which had grown more and more thick and dense as the sun mounted toward the zenith now fairly darkned its noonday glare and the heat became even to the hardiest almost beyond endurance. Then it was that the terrified populace fully appreciated their peril, then and not till then did the terrible race for life begin. Stout hearts grow weak and strong men turn pale at the memory of that hour of mortal agony, when men, women and children seemed doomed to certain death in that veritable hell upon earth.

At twenty minutes to three or forty minutes.

ENGINEER WILLIAM BEST.

after the first alarm was turned in the local freight
on the Eastern Minnesota, from Duluth, Engineer
Ed Barry with a train of thirty emyties and ten loads
pulled into Hinckley. Everything was afire at that
time but the town itself, and the heat and smoke
were intense almost to suffocation. The freight
was side-tracked until the arrival of Passenger
No. 4 from the north at 3:25 with Engineer Best
and Conductor Powers in charge. After a short
consultation with them Engineer Barry ran up
to the other end of the yard and coupled onto three
box cars and the caboose and backed down on
the main track and joined the passenger, making a
train of three box cars, a caboose and five passenger
coaches besides the two engines. All this time the
fire had been pushing on in its mad career and a-
bout this time it was announced by Captain Craig
of the Department to the throng of people gathered at the west end of the town that the fire was
beyond control; that the whole town would soon
be in flames and that they must save themselves
for he could do nothing for them. Then began
the mad rush for life, which has no parallel in the
history of stricken humanity, and it may well be
said that it is our fervent prayer that we may be
spared so terrible an ordeal.

It has been said that "there are moments in all
men's lives that try men's souls." If it be so this
certainly was one of them. Men, women and chil-

dren struggled with one another for that most precious of God's gifts, life. Yet with it all was exhibited a spirit of self sacrifice of the strong in the succor of the weak, and a wonderful exhibition of the noblest attributes of mankind. Heroes were on every hand and heroic deeds were enacted on all sides without number, the details of which will never be known until the Book of the Great Hereafter is opened for our inspection. Men who saw their families safe on board, turned back at the risk of their own lives to carry the helpless children of their freinds to a place of safety. One man carried no less than twenty children out of the fiery furnace in this way, another went through every house left in the town to see that none were left behind and it is a very significant fact that a very large percentage of those who perished in the flames were those best able to take care of themselves but who sacrificed their own lives for the sake of others.

After having escaped from being incinerated in their homes, those who succeeded in boarding the Eastern Minnesota Emergency train placed their lives in the hands of a few men upon whose courage and strength of character rested the great responsibility of carrying them out of danger. Heroes they were, every one of them and it seems to me that their courage, strength and good judgement should not only be commended but should receive a more substantial recognition at the hands of a

CONDUCTOR H. D. POWERS

public which but for their presence of mind would
have heard of a calamity infinitely more horrible
than it is as recorded today. At such a time and
under such circumstances a man must needs be a
a hero to stick to a post of duty and do that duty
in the face of every danger and at the risk of his
own life.   Too much cannot be said of the fortitude of the brave Engineers or of their indomitable
Conductor. To Engineer Best and Conductor Powers, without doubt, belongs the greatest credit, for
saving this train. Engineer Barry, of course, did
his part and did it well, but it was   the superior
judgement of Best and Powers that decided how
long it would be possible to delay the train, and
just when the crucial moment had arrived, when
it was unsafe to stay longer, and too much cannot
be said in the way of commendation of the cool,
clear-sighted and masterful manner in which the
train was handled by the engineers and train-men
in loading the passengers. After waiting at the depot in the heat and smoke for three quarters of an
hour, and until men and animals were falling in
the streets from the heat, at a quarter past four
Best loosened the brakes and the train moved out
across Grindstone bridge toward a place of safety.

After crossing the bridge the train waited five
minutes and took on forty more of the panic strick-
en towns-people, then as the ties under the train
were burning and even the cars themselves were

blistering and almost blazing from the intense heat the train pulled out though in doing so they were obliged to leave men, women and children to that fiery ordeal which meant almost certain death. At the last stop the heat had become so intense that the very rails were begining to warp and twist out of shape with heat.

After having taken on all that could be saved by them the engineers put on all steam and rushed toward a place of safety as fast as the wheels could turn. Everythiug was burning, fire on all sides and the heat continued to be so intense and terrible, that combined with the smoke, it seemed as if those who had gotten on the train would die of suffocation. But it had been willed otherwise and it was not to be. Seven miles out of Hinckley they found for the first time a cool current of air and from that time on they breathed easier. Though they were by no means out of the fire limits the heat did not seem so intense and the smoke was perhaps a little less blinding, although through all the run from Hinckley to Duluth the head-light was kept burning, it having been found necessary at Partridge on the down trip of the freight in the morning.

When through the smoke the engineers could see by their knowledge of the road-bed that a bridge was close by, Best would put on his brakes, his engine controlled the air-brakes of the five passen-

ENGINEER ED. BARRY.

ger coaches which made up the bulk of the train in weight, and slow down to a three or four mile an hour gait, until they were certain the bridge was there when they would pass on. Special mention should be made of the brave deeds of two brakemen, whose names we are sorry to say we were unable to learn, who rode on the back end of Barry's tank, as they backed out, and as they reached a bridge would signal Barry, whether or not it was all right and he in turn would whistle off to Best, when they would go on to the next bridge where the operation was repeated. Nineteen bridges in fourteen miles of road over which they passed were found after the fire to have been totally destroyed and they were all burning more or less furiously when the train passed over them.

When Sandstone was reached the train was pulled up and the people were begged to get aboard and fly for their lives. Some grasped the opportunity but more did not, laboring under the impression that although Hinckley had burned, Sandstone was safe, an impression they had cause to regret an hour later when Sandstone was gutted as completely as Hinckley had been.

Only a short stop was made at Sandstone, when the whistle sounded and the heavily loaded train started again on its way. On reaching Kettle River just out of Sandstone, the bridge was burning and the train slowed up before reaching it when a cry from the watchman "For God's sake, go on, you can cross it now and it will go down in five minutes," made Barry draw a quick breath and with set teeth throw her wide open and run out on the bridge. They crossed in safety as if by a miracle and five minutes later the bridge fell of its own weight.

There were two watchman at the bridge, a young man and one whose hair was tinged with gray. After the train had passed, the clothes of both watchmen were on fire and they started down a ladder by the side of the bridge in order to escape in the waters below. The younger man, whose family were already in the river, being quicker and more agile than his colleague went down first and succeeded in saving himself. While the older one in following was overcome by the heat at the first landing and fearing to go on turned back and climbing to the top again, died at his post on the grade.

By this time the closely huddled passengers after having been exposed to the terrible heat for such a length of time were suffering horrible agony for a drink of water. At Partridge it was found necessary to take twenty minutes in order to get the engines ready to go on, and the time was improved in getting water to the occupants of the cars. Up to this time the train had been running with-

out orders and against the time of a aown freight.
At Partridge Engineer Barry got a message to use
his own judgement and run as he saw fit, coupled
with the information that the down train No. 23
had been abandoned. Like their Sandstone neighbors the people at Partridge refused to leave and
the train pulled out again, stopping at Mansfield
and Kerrick. At Kerrick Engineer Barry found
that his eyes had become so effected by the smoke
and heat that he could scarcely see at all to say
nothing of running an engine with a train load of
people under his charge. He thought he would be
compelled to give up but after about ten minutes
rest, he plucked up courage and ran her through
to West Superior, where he could go no further as
he could see nothing. When he left his engine he
was so exhausted with the heat and smoke and
the mental strain he had been under that he could
not stand but was carried to the Round House and
cared for.

Without wishing to depreciate in any way the
noble deeds of Jim Root and Jack McGowan on the
St. Paul & Duluth, of which so much has been said
in various newspaper reports, it would seem to me
that Engineers Best and Barry of this Emergency
Train displayed courage and good judgment in
facing the heat and backing out of Hinckley equal
in every way to that shown on the south bound
limited and as such should receive equal commend-

ation and recognition of their services. At the time the south bound limited started its run back to Skunk Lake it had no alternative but to go back or be burned, as the bridge across the Grindstone River just north of Hinckley was already burning and was unsafe, while Engineers Best and Barry were obliged to cross a bridge which was similarly situated across the same stream half a mile east of this one, and they waited for more than half an hour knowing the bridge was on fire and upon its strength rested the lives of themselves and their passengers. Yet in the face of all this they waited and tried to get them all.

Near view of mud-hole at Skunk Lake.

CHAPTER IV.

SKUNK LAKE.

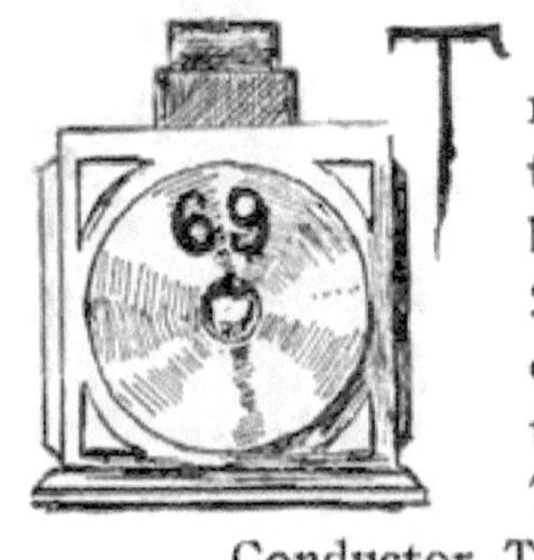

HE south bound limited on the St. Paul & Duluth road left Duluth for St. Paul at 2 o'clock in the afternoon of that eventful Saturday, the first day of September. The train was in charge of

Conductor, Thomas Sullivan,

Engineer, James Root,

Fireman, Jack McGowan

Brakeman, John Monihan,

Baggageman, Geo. F. Morris,

Porter, John Blair,

News Agent, Hermann Mannhart.

Little did they think that in two short hours

time they would be oliged to undergo one of the
most trying ordeals that human beings ever endured and that ere night their names would be
entered on the Roll of Honor as heroes worthy of
the highest tributes of gratitude and commendation it was in the power of humanity to bestow.

The train consisted of one combination car, one
coach, two chair cars and Engine 69. The atmosphere was heavy with smoke even as the train
pulled out of the Duluth Depot and all the way
down to Carlton it grew gradually thicker and
more dense, until at that point it was found to be
necessary to light the head-light and all the lamps
in the train, as the smoke had so darkened and obscured the afternoon sun that it was found necessary, both for safety and comfort to have this artificial light. About this time the passengers began
to show signs of uneasiness, especially among the
women and children, and many a wistful glance
was cast toward the men in the party as ifimplor-
ing assistance and protection from a foe insid ious
and insatiable. Onward swept the ill-fated train,
with its precious cargo of humanity, and but for
the heroism of two men it might have been said
to certain destruction. But James Root and John
McGowan were made of sterner stuff than the ordinary mortal and when the terrible ordeal came
they were tried and were not found wanting.

Steadily, sturdily on they plunged with determi-

CONDUCTOR THOMAS SULLIVAN.

nation depicted in every line of the frame of that
redoubtable engine driver, and his only thought
was to hold out until the fire was passed when all
would be well. He was, with many others laboring under a false impression as to the actual extent
and intensity of the fire and never dreamed that
Hinckley could be burned in this way. Still the
smoke increased and the heat became more and
more intense and insufferable. It filled all the
coaches until it was found difficult to breathe and
of course added much to the dismay of the already
panic stricken passengers. The train men passed
through the cars saying there was nothing to cause
any alarm, that the smoke would soon be past and
imploring the passengers to keep their wits about
them and not give vent to their feelings, though
things might look dubious just then. By this time
however, the train had approached near enough
so that the flames could be seen to the right of the
track and the roar of the blazing demon could be
distinctly heard, so that the quieting words of the
trainmen fell like seeds upon rather stony ground,
and the excitement increased with the moments.
It soon became apparent that they all had but the
slightest chance for their lives, and the scene when
this was realized was terrible to witness. Strong
men turned white and rigid, their set teeth and
drawn lips and the wild look in their eyes showing
the mental strain under which they were passing.

Women screamed and prayed and children clung
to their mothers and cried and screamed, they
knew not why. Abject fear was depicted on all
countenances while a few showed a determination
to make the best of a horrible predicament and to
make as strong a fight for life as was possible.
On, on rumbled the train every instant adding
terror to the scene in the coaches until within a
mile and a half of Hinckley. At this point came
the first information to the train that anything
extraordinary was happening or had happened
at Hinckley. The smoke was so dense it was impossible to see the town and even if it had been
possible the town was shut from view by a high
hill. A number of fleeing, panic-stricken citizens
flagged the train and in a few words told the engineer their story and then with their party boarded the train, about one hundred and fifty or two
hundred people in all were rescued in this way.
Coming as they did from the flames of their homes,
feeling that their lives were hanging by the merest
thread which might snap at any time, smarting
from burns and stifled by the smoke and heat, oft-
times separated from loved ones, whom they would
meet no more in this life, is it any wonder they
lost their self control and boarded the train a gasp-
ing, excited and half-crazed concourse of people?
 The train was within a mile and a half of Hinckley when it was flagged and the fire was coming

towards it with a speed of a locomotive, backed by
that horrible wind. Engineer Root's first impulse
was to put on all speed and run through the fire,
but a second of deliberation caused him to reverse
his engine and run back away from it. Then began a race which has no parallel in history, unless,
perhaps it be the race of the Emergency Train on
the Eastern Minnesota, which at that same instant was running a similar race under similar
circumstances on a track about two miles east of
the scene of this act in the tragedy. No one knows,
no one can have any accurate conception of the
awfulness and the suffering of that horrible ride.
At first Root had no definite destination in view
and no orders to run back on but those of common
sense and humanity; then he thought of a little
marsh lake called Skunk Lake near the track
about four miles from the point where they had
met the refugees and turned back, and this lake he
determined to reach at all hazards as he knew in
doing so lay his only hope of safety or even of life
itself. On and on came the flames and the brave
engineer saw they were rapidly gaining on him
and put on a full head of steam in the hope that
he might distance them, but all to no purpose, the
fiery fiend had marked its prey, and was not to be
baffled by a mere trifle such as a higher rate of
speed. On it came, gaining steadily until it burst
over them in its hurricane blast Smoke and flames

were everywhere. They came in at the ventilators at the top of the car, and through the cracks at the side of the windows. The rear coach was on fire and its passengers more terror stricken and horrified than ever fled to the other coaches to escape from the immediate danger, but the effort proved futile; one after another all the coaches first blistered with the heat and finally commenced to blaze. Then for a few minutes ensued a scene horrible beyond description. The roar of the flame—the stifling suffocation and darkness of the smoke—the intense heat, the shrieks and moans of the poor unfortunates almost baking in those crowded cars, lent to the scene a pandemonium, which it can be readily understood beggars description. ' The heat was so insufferable and intense that it cracked the glass in the windows of the cars, and as it did so, one man, perhaps more excitable than the rest lost his mind, literally went mad, and with a horrible shriek threw himself from one of the windows and was swallowed up in the seething mass of smoke and burning cinders, a-nother and another followed his example and all were caught and destroyed by the insatiable flames.

Imagine if you can the effect upon an already thoroughly frightened and exhausted train load of people of seeing three of their number jump to a death which they verily believed would soon be their own. No power on earth under the circum-

Where the People Were Saved.   Skunk Lake Proper.

stances could have prevented the panic that ensued, and one after another ten more unfortunates
thought death itself preferable to such suspense
continued any longer and threw themselves from
the windows of that ill-fated train.

While these scenes were being enacted in the
coach engineer Root in his cab was suffering terrible agony from the heat. Wrapped in a large
overcoat he kept his seat in the face of all the dangers which beset his path.

Fire everywhere, his hands were blistered by the
heat as he still held the lever, his clothes were burning as were also those of his fireman, Jack Mc-
Gowan. Jack leaped into the manhole of the water-
tank and put out the fire in his own clothes, then
grasping a pail, completely soused Jim with the
contents of the tank; still on they flew, Jim holding
the lever and Jack dashing water over him and
helping him on. The glass in the cab window at
Jim's side burst with the heat and a piece of it
struck him in the neck and cut a horrible gash
close to the jugular vein, and it bled profusely.
Weakened by the loss of blood, the heat and smoke
which he was obliged to endure, and feeling the
terrible responsibility of saving so many human
beings, twice was Jim overcome and fell from his
seat to the cab floor and twice was he bolstered
up by the faithful Jack.

On and on they flew, words cannot describe the

scene, fire and smoke on every side and it seemed
as if the very air was in league with the demon, to
bring upon this frightened train-load death that
comes in this awful form.   To give the reader some
idea of the heat in the cab, it might be said that as
soon as the window burst with the heat the curtain
caught fire and was torn down by Jack McGowan.
The lagging caught fire and in spite of the rapidity
with which they backed up, the flames were more
swift and blew back into the cab, setting the front
of the cab on fire, burning all the wooden handles
of the steam connections, scorching the seats and
melting the cab lamp.

Minutes they were, but they seemed like hours, ere
Skunk Lake was reached and the brave engineer
brought the train to a stand-still and the trainmen pointed out to the terror-stricken passengers
the direction of the lake.   As soon as the lake was
reached McGowan assisted his wounded engineer
to the water, and finding he could be of no assistance to others he laid down in the water himself.
Owing to his superior physical strength he was
able to care for Root and others in his power until the arrival of the Relief train from Duluth.
Throughout the whole run exhibiting a spirit of
heroism and self sacrafice not surpassed in that
awful ordeal, where self sacrafice was not an un-
common occurance and heroes were met on all sides.

This train had on board from one hundred and

PORTER JOHN BLAIR.

thirty-five to one hundred and fifty regular through passengers and took aboard from one hundred and fifty to two hundred refugees from Hinckley. The exact number will probably never be known. Certaiu it is that over three hundred people owe their lives to the little water that remained in that lake, which owing to the continued drought had been reduced to a mere morass of mud and water. Here they lay four mortal hours, their faces close to the muddy water and endeavoring to hold up against the heat and smoke that lay so close to the ground that they were in danger of suffocating. Most of the passengers reached the lake, but some few who became confused and who ran any direction without stopping to think what or where, and when their friends succeeded in quieting them and starting them through the bush toward the lake the trees were all ablaze and the heat was so intense that they were obliged to turn back to the track where they remained until the fire had passed although none actually died from the heat on the tracks.

After the fire had abated a little Root and McGowan went back to the train to see if they could not save the engine and tank. McGowan endeavored to put out the fire in the tank but as the coal was burning he was unable to do so, so they uncoupled her from the tender and ran her ahead a short distance and this saved the engine with comparatively little damage. Root had by this time become thoroughly chilled by lying in the cold water and repaired to the floor of his cab where he was found by the relief.

The only fatalities that actually occured on the train itself were two Chinamen who were on board and who seemed dazed and demented and could not be moved from their seats. They staid there overcome with the heat and burned with the ill-fated train. Then too, were those who threw themselves from the train before it reached Skunk Lake, all of whom perished in the flames.

At the time of the fire the newspapers gave it out that Conductor Thomas Sullivan became confused and wandered aimlessly about and was found the next day about nine miles north of Skunk Lake in a state of mental demoralization. This is, however, not the fact, as soon as he found that his passengers were safe he started back to Miller to protect his train as he knew that a freight was following him or that he was running against the time of the freight and feared that the calamity of a collision would be added to what had already occured- After an awful struggle with the heat he reached the station and sent the message, when true to his trust, that accomplished he was obliged to succumb to the strain. He had done his duty as a man and a hero, human nature could do no more.

Special mention should also be made of the efforts
of Herman Mannhart and J. W. Blair, the book-
agent and porter whose efforts in assisting the
ladies in their escape were self- sacraficing and heroic. Blair taking especial pains and using the
Fire Extinguisher that is carried on the train to
put out the fire that had caught in the ladies dresses.

The gravel pit of the Eastern Minnesota proved to be a God-send to those of the Hinckleyites who were not able to get a-way form the doomed berg on either of the trains, the escape of which has been describ-ed in the preceeding chapters. After the train on the Eastern Minneso-ta had pulled out, those who remained turned to the gravel pit as a last resort, knowing if that fail-ed then all hope would be lost. The gravel pit had been made by the Eastern Minnesota Ry. Co, who had used the gravel for the improvement of their road-bed. It covered some two or three acres of ground and its bottom lay some twenty or thirty feet below the level of the surrounding country, so that those who took refuge here were saved the excruiating suffering of the fierce blast of the wind which was to some extent broken from them. They were however, obliged to endure a constant shower of cinders and burning coals that made life very disagreeable and caused no end of suffering. About seventy people in all, men, women and children sought shelter in this pit. It contained a pool of water about three feet in its greatest depth and closely huddled together in this pool were seventy human beings besides all the domestic animals that survived the fury of the flames, such as horses, cows, pigs, chickens, etc. It proved to be the safest place in Hinckley, three or four hundred trunks which had been carried by the frightened people and hurled over the edge into the pit, where they lay all through the fire, came out unscathed.

A number of vehicles had also been driven into the gravel pit, and in the work of relief that was to come they proved a very efficient means of distribution. The party entered the pit at about seven or eight minutes past four, and remained in the water from two to four hours.

The first twenty minutes of the ordeal is described as being something terrible. The heat was so intense and the smoke so dense and blinding that all were suffering from the burning and smarting of their eyes and writhing from the intense heat, and the men were obliged to constantly throw water over the women and children to keep them from growing faint and falling under the pressure. As most of the occupants of the gravel pit were women and children this duty devolved upon the few men of the party and with this duty and that of wetting cloths and wrapping them about their own heads and those of their proteges the men were kept busy through the entire ordeal. One man whose name could not be learned was overcome by the heat and smoke at the gravel pit, fell into the water and was drowned. As far as is known this was the only fatality in the pit.

This gravel pit was large enough to have saved all the people of Hinckley and all their household goods besides, if they had only sought refuge here, but it was only the cool-headed ones that seemed to think of this or take it into consideration at all as an avenue of escape. The great majority of the people followed their first impulse, which was to fly; anything to get away from the fire and they trusted to their physical strength to keep out of the way of its ravenous advance, a feat which was utterly impossible by mere physical strength alone as was altogether too conclusively demonstrated on the north road.

It is the natural query of any one who is not acquainted with the section, "Why in the world did not all the people run to the Grindstone River, that was only a quarter of a mile, just think some of them were saved a mile and a half from the

The Gravel Pit.

town."The query is very natural and to look upon the map one would imagine a very correct one but it is another illustration of the practical uselessness of a theory. As a matter of fact, the Grindstone River is nothing more nor less at this time of year than a little brooklet and scarcely deserves the dignity of the title of a stream at all. A person could step across it in many places and while it proved a shelter to some of the survivors it was not the shelter that would have been chosen by anyone familiar with the country, who had any choice in the matter. Most of those who plighted their faith with the river did so from sheer desperation not knowing what else to do and quite a number met their death here from one cause or another, either by smoke, being overcome by the heat or by the waters themselves. A notable case of this sort being the wife of Martin Martinson and their three little boys whose little flaxen heads were found wholly unscorched showing they had met their death by the more merciful means of water than the horrible tortures of a fiery entrance into the life beyond.

By far the most heart rending and horrifying scene of the vicinity after the fire had done its deadly work was on the road about a mile north of the town across the Grindstone River. Here in a little swale which had become thoroughly dried by the long continued drought so that at the time of the fire it had absolutely no water in it, were found the bodies of one hundred and twenty six persons, besides a number of horses and cows which probably followed the people out of the town, they too, looking for a place of safety

To look at it now impassionately after it is all over, it is very easy for us to say, "Well, why in the world didn't they go to the River or to the gravel pit? They might have known the fire would overtake them if they attempted to run away from it."

When this is said we must first stop and think that they were weak human beings; that they were fleeing from what they thought they could not possibly escape; some even thinking that it was the judgment day itself; that they had no time for preparation; that they were dismayed and confused by the heat, smoke and roar of the storm and some were actually crazed by the awfulness of the scene. We ourselves placed in a similar position under similar circumstances would perhaps have used even less judgment than was shown by these unfortunates, whose untimely end was so tragic as to wring a sympathetic wail from every quarter of the world where the electric spark and the wire could carry the news.

At the time of the first alarm, when it was known that the town was doomed, and the mad rush to escape began, many horses were harnesed to buggies or to other vehicles and all except a few that sought

THE MARSH WHERE ONE HUNDRED AND TWENTY-SIX PEOPLE DIED.

shelter in the gravel pit, followed out on the north road, as the most natural thing to do. A great many of these refugees boarded either one train or the other of which we have spoken, and in fact had it been possible for the Eastern Minnesota train to wait for this unfortnuate band of one hundred and twenty-six, all might have escaped on this train, as their bodies were found within a few rods of the Eastern Minnesota track and to the right of the wagon road. The party of town people, who flagged Root's train on the St. Paul & Duluth R. R. were the foremost of this contingent who followed out on the north road. For the most they had no definite destination, they had no idea as to what or where they were going, they only knew that it was certain death to remain and while death overtook many of them in their mad rush to escape, their idea was to get as far as possible from that on-coming hurricane of fire. When the unfortnates came to this apparent marsh which many of them knew had held water, they sought it as a last hope, a last resort, and it proved of no avail. They dared not turn back to the river, in fact they could not do so. So they pressed forward to the very center of the slough, where the grass grew thick and rank, hoping against hope that they might find water, which was worth more than all things else beside. They were, however, doomed to disappointment. Their death warrants

had been signed and sealed and the grim warrior
showed no quarter or mercy in their exceution. It
was a fearful sight; no battlefield ever presented
one more shocking or more terribly heart rending.
Huddled together within an area of less than two
acres of ground lay one hundred and twenty-six
human bodies blackened and burned beyond
recognition. All were more or less distoited and
most of them seemed to be in exactly the same position and to show the sad expressions of their
emotions and terrible sufferings they were undergoing when the first wave of heat swept over them.
When they inhaled its horrible gases and met death
as instantaneously as they might have done in the
electric chair of a New York sheriff of the most
approved and latest pattern. That death came
instantaneously to most of them, there can be no
possible question or doubt, as this fact is conclusively proven both from the posture of their bodies
after the fire and the condition in which they were
found.

For instance, a young girl was found kneeling
with her hands clasped, palms together and face
turned upward showing that her last breath had
murmured a prayer. A number showed that the
victims had been in motion when over-taken and fell
with the muscles in exactly the same position as
they were the instant the fire had reached them,
not having even relaxed and fallen limp. One of

the most gruesome features of the scene being the appearance of the victims who were almost invariably without any vestige of clothing except perhaps the soles of the shoes, and were in many cases burned beyond any possibility of recognition and where recognition was possible it was difficult from the blistering of the skin and singeing of the hair, which gave a most uncanny appearance to a sight, ghastly even under the most auspicious circumstances. One noticeable fact in connection with this band of unfortunates is that they were made up mostly of the most ignorant classes of the town. Those who had not the mental capacity to appreciate anything more than the fact that they were in great danger and this one thought seemed to force all others from their minds even to the exclusion of a thought of how that danger was to be averted and to this fact, perhaps more than anything else, can be laid the responsibility of such an enormous loss of life in this one spot. Most of the better classes of the Hinckleyites, the store-keepers and professional men got away on one of the two trains, nearly all though, escaped by the Eastern Minnesota.

Another feature which proved misleading and gave to some a mistaken idea of what the fire actually was, until it was too late, was the roar of the hurricane. Many people mistook its approach for the coming of a cyclone and fled to their cellars a place of all places where they were almost sure to be cremated with their buildings. Others took refuge in wells and root cellars which had been covered with earth and were thus protected from the fury of the elements, and in this way they escaped, but it is certainly a sad tale where thirteen people were taken from a well where they had been suffocated by the heat.

CHAPTER VI.

SANDSTONE, PARTRIDGE, SANDSTONE JUNCTION, POKEGAMA AND MISSION CREEK.

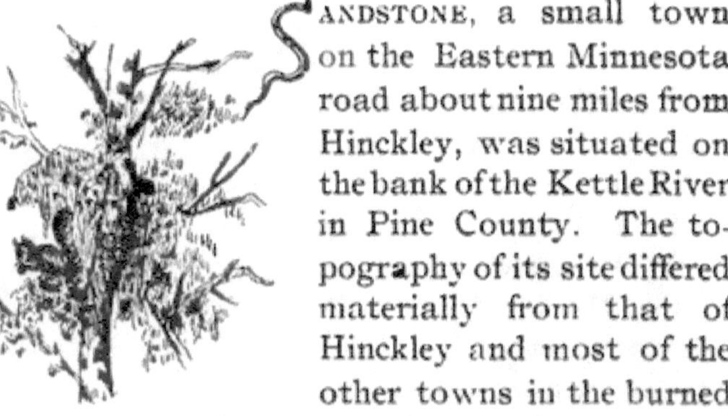

ANDSTONE, a small town on the Eastern Minnesota road about nine miles from Hinckley, was situated on the bank of the Kettle River in Pine County. The topography of its site differed materially from that of Hinckley and most of the other towns in the burned section in that it lay on a high bluff which was marked and seamed with great ravines; and too it also differed in that it depended to a great extent upon the product of the quarries in this bluff for its support. These quarries were quite extensive and from them Sandstone takes its name. The Kettle River at this point is a stream of no small dimensions being from three hundred to four hundred feet in width even at this time, when the drouth had been so pronounced and prolonged that the entire

country seemed parched with the heat.   The people
of Sandstone like those of Hinckley, were in no
way alarmed on the morning of the eventful Saturday September 1st, 1894. The good wife went
steadily about her house-hold duties, making the
cake, baking the bread and preparing perhaps for
a quiet little family excursion on the morrow
when if the day were pleasant and everything pro-
pitious she could have a little time for a quiet chat
with her better half, and enjoy a little outing a-
mong the woods and rocks along the river bank.
Peace, quiet and harmony on all sides, save perhaps, when the blast from the quarry reverberated
along the distant bluffs as the good-wife's man
toiled with his companions in their somewhat perilous task of tearing from its bed the rock that
brought food for his little ones and shelter for his
loved ones. No thought of danger had crossed
their minds, nor did they appreciate that they
were in any danger when the Emergency Train under Enginners Best and Barry pulled into the Depot.
There was the usual number of loungers gathered
there to see the train come in and see if they had by
any chance received a letter or package in the mail
pouch. They were of course surprised to see four
hundred and seventy rescued citizens of Hinckley
fleeing from their homes, and while their town was
then surrounded by fire, and the smoke was so
thick and dense that it was difficult to breath, and

THE BRIDGE AT SANDSTONE.

their vision was obscured, they scorned the idea
that Sandstone was doomed to the same fate that
her sister city just nine miles away had suffered,
and for the most part refused to take the proffered
aid in time and escape when the opportunity was
offered them. In vain did those who knew what it
was to escape death in its awful form entreat them
to fly for their lives. They refused to heed the
warning and the train was obliged to pull out and
leave them to their fate, and in less than half an
hour from that time, the hurricane of fire had done
its deadly work, and of Sandstone nothing remained but heaps of ashes here and there except
one small building which from its position in the
quarry escaped the ruin, and sixty-three of the
towns-people had perished in the flames. They
doubted, and it was their doubt that proved their
ruin, they had been warned and had that warning
been heeded not a single death need have been
chronicled in the history of the fire at Sandstone.
They remained at the Depot until the Fiery Demon
was in sight, coming on with the speed of a race
horse, then they realized the truth that had been
told them and endeavored to make amends for
their negligence in the mad rush for safety into the
waters of the Kettle River. They were none too
soon and their mad rush gave them no time to
warn only those who happened to be on the one
main street in the town, all others being left to

their fate; that first law of life, the law of self
preservation being too strong to admit of any delay
in the matter of reaching the river bank. A number of unfortunates hearing the roar of the storm
and mistaking its real nature for that of a cyclone,
fled to the only place of safety against such a calamity, the cellar, and found themselves in the
place of all others from which there was no possible means of escape, and when relief arrived they
were found in their own homes burned beyond any
possibility of recognition. As was the case in the
entire fire swept district, narrow escapes among
the survivors were the rule rather than the exception, instances of heroic self-sacrifice could be cited
by the hundred and an attempt to record them all
would require a hundred books the size of this volume, and even then it could truly be said that
"the half had never been told." When the sun rose
at Sandstone on that Sunday morning after the
fire it shone upon as desolate and sad a scene as
was ever spread before it, ruin and dire desolation
every-where, and eveything lay black with smoke
and charred with fire or was still smoking as some
substance more substantial than the rest eked out
its fight for existence a few hours longer than its
neighbors. Near the station lay the form of a woman black and ghastly and charred beyond all
possibility of being recognized, and ten rods farther
on toward the river lay her husband, face down-

ward, the only vestige of clothing on his body being a heavy pair of shoes. About thirty rods nearer the river was the form of a sturdy twelve year old lad who had fallen fighting manfully for life, and a little farther back on the road from the woman was the body of another child, who had been the first to fall. A few hours before these four had occupied a little farm-house about half a mile south of Sandstone, and comprised all the members of a family by the name of Broad, who had run for the river, but had been overcome by the heat and fallen and died on the road in the order named. Their buildings were also burned and of this farmer and his happy family and home, nothing is now left but a heap of ashes. Another farmer, one Louis Matas had a narrow escape. He saw the fire coming and made every preparation to give it battle but finding his efforts worse than futile he gave it up and took refuge in a well. He carried a bundle of clothes with him and descended by a ladder to the bottom of this well. There were several feet of water in the well, but even then with its protection he suffered intensely from the heat; and the sparks together with the heat, set fire to and actually burned the clothing he had carried down with him and attempted to save. All of the survivors at Sandstone owe their lives and their escape to the fact that they were able to reach the river, where they waded in up to their necks and then only saved themselves by keeping their faces and heads constantly wet by throwing water upon each other. The next morning the survivors some one hundred people went to Hell's Gate, a point about four miles from Sandstone on the Kettle River where they were fed supper by a man by the name of Place where they remained until about one oclock in the morning, when two messengers arrived saying that the relief train on the St. Paul & Duluth was at Sandstone Junction four miles away, and wishing them to walk to the train. This they did, men, women and children, four miles over burnt stumpage on a dark night is no small undertaking, yet in all the distance not a single complaint was heard nor even a whimper from a child, all were so grateful for this miraculous deliverance that their hearts were too full for utterance.

Partridge was only a small station, a mere sidetrack with a few buildings on the Eastern Minnesota Railway, about six miles above Sandstone. The whole population of the town did not exceed fifty people and of these only one death is known; he bears the romantic and time-honored name of Robert Burns, and was burned to death. At the time the Eastern Minnesota train passed through Partridge they stopped and endeavored to induce the people to get aboard, but they all refused and did not go but in twenty minutes time were compelled to seek some place of refuge. They had no river or gravel pit to fall back upon, so the women and children were placed upon hand-cars and were hastily taken up the road about three miles to a lumber camp where about one hundred acres had been burned over. In this oasis the refugees staid from a little before six until twelve o'clock at night when they were rescued by the relief train from West Superior. Five families constituted the entire population of Partridge and all the residents made their escape into this clearing, the women and children being carried on the hand-cars and some of the men walking the entire distance. The town of Partridge was totally destroyed there being nothing whatever saved from the fury of the conflagration.

Sandstone Junction or Miller was another mere station on the St. Paul & Duluth road rine miles north of Hinckley. It never boasted of the dignity of a post-office nor did Partridge for that matter, but was merely a side-track for lumber Most of the residents of the section were farmers who had made clearings and settled on them. Most of these that escaped did so either by getting into a well or a potato patch and covering themselves with earth in order to protect themselves from the heat. Quite a number of the settlers were away at the time but about fifty per cent of those who were there were burned to death.

Pokegama: Circumstances were such that the

survivors of fire at Pokegama suffered more actual pain from the heat, than those in any other section of the burned district. That this is a fact there can be no question. Pokegama is a small station on the Eastern Minnesota Railway about seven miles south of Hinckley on Pokegama Creek, a small stream never more than twelve feet in width but at this time completely dried up so that no water remained in it except an occasional pool deeper than the rest of the bed of the brook. The wind at Pokegama was noticed to freshen at about ten o'clock in the morning and at twelve o'clock the fire reached the west side of the town and burned everything that was burnable in that direction. About two o'clock the fiery hurricane reached Pokegama and so fierce and rapid was its onslaught that nothing whatever could be saved and it was as if by a miracle that the people were saved themselves. A good many of the settlers in the viciuity came into town at the first alarm of fire, and those who did not, did not live to tell the story of their sufferings. Thirty of the residents of this sention fled to Pokegama creek, and laid there in the water until the fire had passed. They took refuge in the sluice-way of the pond at Pokegama's mill and these suffered excruciating agony from the heat. They were in a veritable oven. The bank on one side of the pond was piled with logs to a depth of fifteen or eighteen feet. The mill, with its refuse and **saw-dust** flanked another side while the third was enclosed by a railroad trestle and bridge one hundred and **eighty feet long** built entirely of wood and inflamable material.

All of these **were entirely** consumed and during all the time that **they were** burning these people laid in the water and endured that intense heat. They all owe their lives to the fact that all this material did not burn at one time, that is, that the logs were pretty well consumed before the mill caught fire, and the mill was burned before the bridge reached its hottest blaze. Twenty-two people are known to have lost their lives in this immediate vicinity. An incident that should be spoken of in this connection is in regard to a train on the St. Cloud branch of the Eastern Minnesota; Which left Hinckley for St. Cloud about half past two of that eventful afternoon. When it reached a point about a mile from Pokegama the rails had spread by the heat and the train left the track on a little two-foot fill. There was only one passenger on board besides the trainmen. Great credit is due the trainmen of this train for their efforts in saving the train from total destruction although the heat was intense and the coaches caught fire repeatedly, cushions smoked and blazed and had to be thrown out to burn, still they kept up their unequal fight carrying water from the tender and standing guard until the danger was past. It would seem singular that this train should escape cremation while Root's train on the St. Paul & Duluth was totally consumed and the only explanation that can be given is that the fire had burst over the vicinity where the train was derailed and gone on some time before the accident occured, so that the trainmen did not have the full fury of the fire to fight. Considerable apprehension was felt among the sufferers at Pokegama lest this train which was expected at any time, should run out on the bridge, which was unsafe even at the time the train came to its unceremonious standstill, and precipitate its passengers to certain destruction. About eight o'clock in the evening the train-crew made its way to Pokegama, and took the blinded and suffering survivors with them back to the derailed and rescued train where they remained until relief arrived.

We append herewith a descriprion of the fire at Mission Creek by one of the survivors, thinking that we cannot improve on the tale as told in his own words.

"Mission Creek, a small town on the St. P. & D. R. R. south of Hinckley had a narrow escape. Standing on the little hill in the center of our small berg on the forenoon of September 1st, large clouds of smoke could be seen rising from brush burning to the south-west. Our people had sniffed smoke all summer and were little alarmed, if any, at this

usual sight.   The light breeze blowing in the morning grew stronger as the hours went by until at
twelve o'clock a hurricane was bearing down upon us from the direction of the fire. A solid mass
of dry pine choppings and underbrush, augmented
here and there with a few hundred tons of hay,
furnished ample food for the hungry hell which was
approaching. The settlers came in to the station
for protection as they had fears that the wind
might drive the fire upon them on their little claims.
We commenced fighting the flames early, but the
effort to quench them was futile. At half past two
the St. Paul & Duluth south-bound passenger went
past the station, but none of our people left. The
train couldn't have gone half a mile from the depot
when a roaring wall of fire bore down on our little
hamlet. The fifty people were taken to Laird &
Boyle's potato patch south of the depot. The
patch contains only two acres, but it afforded a
safe, though excessively hot, refuge for our band.
Everyone laid face downward in the furrows, and
the fire swept over to the houses and mill property.
The refuges remained in their trying positions until the fire had swept everything in sight and passed
on to its work of death and destruction to the
north. We took a retrospective view of the situation which met us, but could do nothing, so proceeded to make ourselves as comfortable as possible.
The section men arrived on the scene in a few hours

time. They brought with them a fine large deer which became entangled in the barbed wire fence while fleeing before the fire and had died there. We dug potatoes and with the welcome venison ate a hearty supper. Excepting the pain in our eyes, none were suffering from the effect of the heat and smoke. Our party went to Pine City on the work train in the evening. The loss of property at Mission Creek was heavy, but the place was fortunate as being the only one wiped out of existence in which the mortuary list does not roll up a large percentage of the population.

CHAPTER VII.

THE FIRE IN WISCONSIN

A T the time the fire fiend was advancing with such rapid strides upon Hinckley and her sister towns in Minnesota, similar scenes were being enacted in a similar fashion about sixty miles east of Hinckley on the line of the Omaha road in Wisconsin. It is needless for me to go into details in the description of the fire itself in this section of the country lying between Cumberland and Ashland. The same hurricane wind was experieneed, the same wave of heat that has been heretofore described, and the fiend advanced upon the unsuspecting inhabitants with the same stride of almost incredible rapidity.

One difference or, I might say, one characteristic, which was rather more noticeable in the eastern fire, was that the fire burned in strips, leaving a mile or two of unburned forest which **lay not** directly in the path of the wind which carried **its** blaze directly in front of it. So that through the entire section which is shown on the map as the fire district, perhaps one-fourth or one-third of the area has not been burned over, but has been burned around and left like an oasis in a desert.

The region affected by the fire in Wisconsin, was what might readily be termed new country. Very little of it was settled at all and what few settlements there were had been made in the last decade.

Lumber was, of course, as yet the principal produce of the region and the lumber interests had built the railroads and developed the country. An immense amount of timber had annually been cut and shipped from the section, and of late years the grain and hay products were of no small importance. The soil was a little sandy but the pine land is good strong soil and will raise, under ordinary conditions, good fair crops of all the small grains as well as vegetables, berries etc., and quite a little of the husbandman's attention had been given to horticulture although the country was not yet old enough to permit of the raising of these products to a very great extent.

While it is true that the greatest loss of life from fire was felt in Minnesota, it is also true that the greatest area was burned over in Wisconsin.

The origin of the eastern blaze is not generally

known. It was, however, in the region a little to the north-west of Rice Lake and north-east from Cumberland. Neither of these two burgs were injured to any great extent but both were close enough to the fire to feel its heat and become alarmed at its awful power.

Barronett was a village of about five hundred people, on the Chicago, St. Paul, Minneapolis & Omaha railroad, about eight miles from Cumberland on Vermillion river. Most of the houses in the town as well as the store etc., were owned by the Barronett Lumber Co., part of the Weyerhauser syndicate who owned and operated a large mill at Barronett. At a few minutes after two o'clock the afternoon of Sept. 1st, two passenger trains, due at Barronett at two o'clock, where they met and passed each other, were standing on the track. They were both a little late on that day and for once, at least, it was fortunate for the people of the town that they were. The smoke and heat had been steadily increasing until when the trains arrived the people had become thoroughly alarmed and were ready and willing to grasp any opportunity which would take them out of danger. As soon as it became apparent that the town was doomed the men in charge of the company's store threw the doors wide open and told the inhabitants to help themselves. A few availed themselves of the opportunity but most of them had their hands full in escaping themselves and seeing that their families were in a place of safety. All, with the exception of a very few, some three or four men got aboard either one train or the other and escaped, with, in most cases, what clothes they had on their backs, and nothing more.

Most of the residents of Barronett were mill hands, never forehanded and usually rather poor than otherwise. Most of the people went south to Cumberland, a few to Shell Lake and a few more to Spooner. Only one life was lost in Barronett, a man by the name of Aleck Erickson staid behind to fight the fire and after it had passed was found lying face downward, where he had been overcome by the heat, within twenty feet of his own door.

In an interview with one F. S. Staub, overseer of the mill of the Barronett Lumber Co., he stated he was one of the men who staid in Barronett through the entire mælstrom of fire. He was running the pump of the mill and staid by as long as possible, when he filled the boilers full of water and with a companion ran for the ditch beside the railroad track where they staid until the next morning before they dared to emerge or move about among the ruins. He stated that the fire reached the town at about half-past two and at a quarter past three there was nothing left but heaps of glowing ashes scattered here and there, which marked the spots where the houses or lumber piles had been only such a short time before.

Shell Lake, Wisconsin, on the Omaha road about eighteen miles north of Cumberland had perhaps as a town the narrowest escape that is to be chronicled. The smoke had been thick all the morning and as the afternoon came on, the fire was seen approaching the town and it was met by the towns-people and kept at bay in the woods about half a mile south of the town until five o'clock, when in spite of the combined efforts of the towns-people it crept into the Shell Lake Lumber Co.'s hay meadow and then it fairly leaped until it had crossd the wagon road. Here it was met by a most stubborn resistance and the efforts of the fire-fighters were here crowned with success and the fire was kept away from the south side of the town, thus saving from destruction the entire business portion of the town and an immense amount of property from the flames. There were no fatalities at Shell Lake. In all there were fifty-three buildings burned and $100,000 worth of property destroyed.

One incident which took place at Shell Lake deserves to be recorded in a book higher than this, where all the good deeds are shown. It seems at the time of the approach of the fire, a widow, a Mrs. Tawney, fifty-three years of age, was living in the part of the town which was in the immed-

iate danger from the flames, her son, a lad of nineteen was very sick with typhoid fever at the time,
and the mother, who had acted as nurse all through
his illness would not leave the bedside of her boy.
When it became apparent that the house was
actually going, she wrapped him in a blanket and
taking him in her arms carried him into the garden
where she laid him and carried water in a dinner
pail (the only thing she had saved from the house)
and kept his clothes and her own from burning
and also used it to carry water to put out the blaze
as it started in her barn. She kept her vigil by the
boy's side in the garden until about mid-night,
when feeling sure that the barn was safe she carried him in there, where he remained until relief
was brought to them. A deed of heroism not
surpassed even in this section where heroes and
heroines were so plenty.

Comstock, another station on the Omaha road
south of Cumberland, scarcely deserving the name
of a town at all, was completly wiped out, not a
single building of any description being left in the
place. The loss to Comstock and to the farming
community adjacent to it is estimated at $75,000.

Cable is a small town on the Omaha road in
Bayfield County. It laid directly in the path of
the fire and was almost totally destroyed by the
flames. Cable is quite a railroad town, being on
the top of a steep grade, and is known among rail-

road men as "the top of the hill" in pulling heavy trains from Bayfield. Its loss was thirteen houses and a railroad building. It had a population of two hundred people and was about one hundred and fifty miles from St. Paul. Heyward was not touched by the flames nor was the country adjacent to it.

Drummond, in Bayfield County about ten miles north of Cable, was in the center of a heavy strip of timber but for some reason was not even scorched by the flames. In passing through on the line of the Omaha road, the oasis at Drummond is quite a noticeable feature, the fire having practically destroyed everything around it while nothing in its immediate vicinity is harmed in the least.

With the exception of Barronett, Mason probably suffered more severely from the fire than any point on the Omaha road. Mason was a live town of five or six hundred people, one hundred and seventy-six miles from St. Paul. It is the junction of the C. St. P. M. & O. R. R. and the D. S. Sh. & Atl. R. R. The town was almost totally destroyed by the fire, the large saw mill and plant, together with a large amount of lumber of the White River Lumber Co., was totally destroyed together with all the other buildings in the town with the exception of the depot and one or two dwellings which alone remain to mark the spot where Mason had stood. Mason was a timber town being almost

exclusively dependent upon the lumber interests
for its support.   Benoit Station or Peck, between
Mason and Ashland was almost totally destroyed.

Ashland itself had a very narrow escape from
being burned in part at least. The fire advanced
within the city limits and the fire department was
kept very busy for some time in saving the town.
The smoke was very dense for several days, and at
the time the fire was at its height the boats on
the lake did not dare to leave their docks, and the
din of their fog-horns and whistles was something
almost deafening.

Washburn, across the bay from Ashland did
not escape entirely unscathed, in fact, had a very
close call from being totally destroyed. Smoke
had hung heavy over the town for several days
and when the flames actually came up to the edge
of the town, every one was on the alert and volunteer fire fighters were plenty. The wind was
blowing a perfect gale, but in spite of that fact the
fire was kept in check for some time, when suddenly fire was discovered in Cook & Co's. Dock
No. 3 or the one farthest north. It having caught
from a spark from the fire south of the town. It
was discovered in good season, and steps were
immediately taken to fight it, but in the terrific
wind it spread through those piles of lumber with
the speed of a race horse, and it was impossible to

get to work in time to keep the flames from spreading to Bigelow & Co's. Docks. This company has four large lumber docks at Washburn, and almost in less time than it takes to tell it, all four were one huge sheet of flame. Fifteen million feet of lumber makes a bonfire larger than is usually seen, and eye-witnesses describe the burning of these lumber docks as one of the most magnificent spectacles that was ever witnessed. Finding their efforts to save the docks were useless the firemen made a heroic fight to save Bigelow & Co's. mill, and their efforts in this direction were successful so that Washburn's loss was confined exclusively to these lumber docks. When the flames were at their height Ashland sent an engine and hose to the assistance of Washburn, and had it not been for this fact it is altogether probable that the whole town would have been destroyed.

At Parishville 500,000 feet of lumber together with Kennedy's mill were burned. Dynamite was used to prevent the spreading of the flames to adjacent plants, and by this means the fire was confined to Kennedy's yard.

Just how much damage was done in this section by the fire it is impossible to determine; and it is difficult for one to have any accurate conception of extent of the calamity and of how general and severe were its effects. Hardly a village in the whole region known as Northern Wisconsin escaped from its ravages, all having been injured to a greater or less extent, and the fire even found its way across the State line into Gogebec and Ontonagon Counties in Northern Michigan. The damage to the railroad companies in the loss of bridges, telegraph poles, ties, fences, etc., is simply enormous. It is almost a wonder that they succeeded in resuming their train service as soon as they did. All were utterly demoralized after the fire had passed and all communication was shut off for a time along all the lines.

A huge trestle three-quarters of a mile in length on the Duluth South Shore and Atlantic was burned at Marengo, which will cripple that road more or less for some time.

Iron River, a thriving town of about 700 people on the Northern Pacific Railroad, midway between Duluth and Ashland had a narrow escape, and even as it was lost eighteen or twenty dwellings and a saw-mill. The inhabitants had expected something of the sort and were prepared to fight, but for a time they were fighting almost against hope. Brule suffered from the fire. An immense amount of damage being done in the magnificent tracts of pine lands along the Brule River, and numbers of homestead shanties and lumber camps with their contents being totally destroyed. Port Wing and Clevedau are also extensive losers from the fire fiend.

Granite Lake is a station on the Omaha road between Barronett and Cumberland and met a similar fate as that of her sister town Barronett almost simultaneously. No loss of life is reported but considerable loss of property in the shape of lumber, buildings, etc., aggregating in all some $50,000. All the inhabitants with their Barronett neighbors escaped to Cumberland.

The following is a list of towns more or less affected by the fire not already mentioned: Phillips, Prentice, Winchester, Fifield, Park Falls, Butternut, Glidden, Miller, High Bridge, Plummer and Iron Belt, Ironwood, Hurley, Gile, Saxon, Odanah, Sanborn, Marengo, Sedgwick, Bayfield, Houghton, Ashland Junction, Moquah, Ino, Poplar, Itasca, Pratt, Agnew and Altamont.

On September 6th, five days after the first inception of the great fire, rain fell over the entire burned district, and where the fire had not already burned everything inflamable, it put a quietus upon it, which kept it from spreading further, and the more copious rains which followed in the next few days effectually checked the flames. This timely shower was welcomed by all, both for the quietus it put on the fire and on account of the crops which were suffering from a lack of moisture.

From High Bridge on the Wisconsin Central road comes a story sad indeed. The family of Isaac Towney, consisting of himself, his wife and five children besides his son-in-law Bargron, who had married Towney's oldest daughter only a short time before, and had taken up his abode with his wife in a cabin only a short distance from the paternal roof. On the morning before the fire Towney, Bargron and a neighbor named McLean had been fighting fire and had endeavored to save Towney's hay and some 4,000 cedar posts which he had cut ready for market. When the fire came the neighbor was some distance from the Towney family and made an attempt to reach his own home, but finally reached the railroad track and lying down in the ditch escaped with his life. The Towney's were not so fortunate however. Within twenty feet of the house was a fifty foot well, containing a foot or two of water at the time of the fire. Into this well were thrown feather beds, blankets, etc., and all the members of the Towney family proceeded to get into what they supposed to be a place of safety, but which proved to be a veritable oven from which there was no escape. When they were taken out their bodies had been burned to a crisp, not a limb remaining to any of the trunks and the whitened skulls of the younger members demonstrating the degree of heat to which they had been subjected. It is more than probable though that death came to them in the more merciful form of suffocation, than from that of the heat itself.

Although Wisconsin was not called upon to provide for but few refugees as compared to her sister State, her Governor, Mr. Peck, immediately issued a proclamation to the citizens under his jurisdiction, stating the facts and asking that voluntary contributions be sent to Col. W. J. Boyle, Secretary of the Relief Committee at Milwaukee. Col. Boyle was secretary of a similar commission which had been appointed to render a similar service at the time the town of Phillips was destroyed a month previous to this time. Steps were immediately taken to furnish relief to those in need, both temporarily and permanently, and it can truly be said that Wisconsin was not behind her neighbor in furnishing the wherewithal to care for her afflicted.

Registration showed about two hundred destitute people at Ashland and as many more at Cumberland and Spooner, together with some at Superior. All were adequately provided for by contributions received from all sources, although some little dissatisfaction was expressed by the committee at the action of Gov. Peck in issuing a manifesto stating that Wisconsin was able to take care of her own, and needed no outside assistance the feeling being that he did not fully appreciate or understand the condition of the destitute sufferers.

CHAPTER VIII

AFTER the first frenzied onslaught of the fire had passed and the suffering survivors dared leave their place of refuge and endeavor to find either their friends or some trace whereby it would be possible to determine where they had been and how it had fared with them; a sight of desolation met their eyes which is better imagined than described. Many of them feared to leave their asylum until the gray of the morning dawned when they came out more dead than alive, smarting from burns, blinded with smoke and faint from hunger and exhaustion.

Desolation, bleak and unbending, nothing but ashes, stumps and remains of individuals less formate than themselves lay on all sides. Everywhere in every direction could be seen nothing but the ravages of the flames. They had no idea of the extent of the loss of life until morning dawned when the daylight brought a realization of the magnitude and awfulness of the disaster and what a narrow thread had held them to this earthly existance, and the appreciation made them fairly sick at heart. They could not speak, no one could utter a word, God in his infinite goodness seemed to have literally tempered the wind to the shorn lambs, and they went about in a half-dazed condition without the appreciation or realization of sights which would under ordinary circumstances have brought tears to the eyes and melted a heart of stone. And had it not been for the generous and timely assistance and relief that was accorded from the outside world their condition would have indeed been much more serious than ever, and would have multiplied in ten fold ratio as the hours went by. They had in truth, been saved from a death by fire, but most of them escaped with only the clothes on their backs.

As has been stated, the people of Hlnckley had no idea of the immense fatality of the fire. When they came out of the gravel pit the prevailing idea was that there had been but little loss of life. They knew that a great number of people had been saved by the Eastern Minnesota train, and when Mr.

Al. Frazer came from the dry marsh and reported the awful calamity that had happened there, they could hardly believe it. Mr. Frazer even, under-estimated the loss, as he reported that there were as many as forty people burned to death in the marsh. Subsequent developments however showed the number to be one hundred and twenty-six.

The sight of ninety-six bodies piled up in one heap ready for burial, all charred and burned beyond recognition and all destined for one common grave, was one that can never be forgotten by those who took part in the interment. The manner of burial will be refered to later under the head of reminiscences where we print Mr. Webber's experiences at the fire.

Everything available in any way, either as food or clothing had been consumed and the long night of suffering and exposure was something terrible to be considered, to the women and children who were not used to what is termed here in the West "roughing it," but had been accustomed to all the luxuries of a civilized home.

No comparison can be made of this and other great calamities of a fiery nature. In the Chicago fire there was a place of safety; somewhere to go and plenty of food and provision for all the sufferers; but here there was no alternative but to go through the fiery furnace and even those whose bodies were immersed in water were burned and scorched about the head and face and suffered terrible agony from breathing the over-heated atmosphere.

All of the survivors tell the same story. "The very air seemed to be ablaze." At the gravel pit the Presbyterian pastor at Hinckley found half a dozen half burned water-melons and they were devoured eagerly by the famished people while his estimable wife, milked one of the cows, that had taken refuge in the pit and the little milk obtained served to keep body and soul of the little ones in the pit together until morning, or until relief arrived. After a little time the water tank at the Eastern Minnesota Round House was discovered to be left standing and the water here obtained helped to alleviate the sufferings of the bereaved people.

The first actual news of the holocaust at Hinckley received by the outside world was taken to Pine City by several of those who had escaped in the gravel pit. They took a hand-car and started toward their destination, and after much labor caused by twisted rails, burned culverts and fallen trees, the party succeeded in reaching Pine City at about eleven o'clock in the evening of the Saturday that the fire occured, and in less than twenty-four hours from the time the fire burst upon them, the citizens of St. Paul and Minneapolis had a train loaded with provisions, clothing and everything

conceivable, necessary for the immediate alleviation
of the wants of the suffering people at the scene of
the disaster, manned by a number of the most active and prominent citizens and physicians of the
two cities. They were however not the first to arrive upon the scene nor the first to respond to the
call for aid. Pine City was first appealed to and
she responded nobly to supply the wants and ne-
cessities her sister city was in such dire need of.

The news that Hinckley was totally destroyed
spread like wild fire and every individual resident
of Pine City prepared in some way to assist in the
alleviation of the sufferings of the unfortunate survivors. The St. Paul & Duluth Railroad had a
train waiting to get through to Hinckley at the
earliest possible moment, and upon this train was
taken everything possible in the way of food, clothing and anything that mind could conceive would
be useful or available in the awful extremity which
had been brought upon this unfortunate band of
people. About half of the population of the town
of Pine City were on board, some as mere cur-
iosity seekers but more to do what could be done
in adding balm to the wounded spirits they were
soon to meet.

The advance toward Hinckley was necessarily
slow, as every little culvert had to be re-built and
repaired and oft-times it was found necessary to
drive an ocasional spike beside the rail before it

was deemed safe for the train to pass over it. So after a very slow and tedious journey through the darkness of the night and the still smoking ruins the relief train reached Hinckley at about three o'clock in the morning.

Dante's Inferno could not have presented a more horrible and heart-rending spectacle than was laid before the eyes of these Pine City citizens on their errand of mercy. The air was still heavy with smoke and the heat was still quite noticeable. Everything was dark save where the coal docks of the railroad companies had stood and these presented a peculiarly bright and lurid glare against the dark back-ground of the blackened earth and darkened sky, as the stock of coal kept in them burned itself out.

They immediately set to work among the ruins to feed the survivors, find the injured and get them aboard the train where they could be taken to a place of safety, and better facilities could be afforded for their care and comfort than was possible here. Most of the survivors who could walk now congregated in the only building left standing at Hinckley save the water-tank house on the Eastern Minnesota Railway. Parties had begun to come in from the surrounding country. Now and again a straggling one alone, too often the only one left to tell the tale of the sufferings of a family; again in bunches of two or three or even

more as some family more fortunate than the rest
had kept the flock together and had escaped the
fury of the flames. All were more or less injured,
few had scarcely any clothes on their backs, all
were nearly blinded from smoke and heat, and fairly
famished from hunger and thirst. A great many
had saved their lives by lying in some muddy pool
and what the fire left undone to add to their general look of despondent delapidation had been accomplished by the mud and water which had
streaked and begrimmed their bodies and faces till
it was difficult to recognize even the best of friends
under the circumstances. And the sight of the
dead was far more ghastly and revolting than the
visage of the living.

Death on all sides. The grim reaper was no re-
specter of persons. All classes were represented
among his victims. Lying where they fell, most of
them in an attitude which would tend to show the
awful anxiety of the moment either for their own
safety or that of a loved one. Cases were frequent where the positions of the bodies showed
conclusively that the unfortunates had met death
with their dying thoughts ones of anxiety, not
for themselves, but for the loved ones they
would protect from all possible harm. Hastily
taking in a survey of the situation the members of
the relief board went to work with a will, for
work was plenty and there was enough to be done

The ruins of the Court House.

to keep all willing hands busy for days. Knowing
that the dead were beyond their help they directed
their energies to seeking out and caring for the injured. After all that could be taken aboard had
been placed on the train, with a part of the Pine
City relief corps, it pulled back to Pine City, taking
out the first load of the survivors who actually
went through the whole of the fire.

Immediately upon the arrival at Pine City of the
train loaded with the wounded survivors, the
skating rink was turned into an impromptu hospital and the lower part of the Knights of Pythias
Hall in the town was used as a cook-house for the
sufferers. The ladies of Pine City, young and old
came to the front as with one impulse, to do what
they could to relieve the afflicted, and they did not
relax their vigil until the responsibility had been
lifted from their shoulders, and the sufferers were
either able to take care of themselves or had been
otherwise provided for. A number of them staid
at their post by the cook stove all Saturday
night so that they had a good warm breakfast,
sufficient to supply all of the hundreds of unfortunates who were brought to Pine City the morning
after the fire. By Sunday noon every person who
had been brought out of the fire district had been
properly fed and cared for, with the assistance of
Rush City which had come in to bear her share of
the burden in the shape of provisions, and with

her staff of surgeons, who proved very efficient in their endeavors to allay the smarting and burning of the blistered epidermis. While this was going on the work of bringing in and burying the dead was being pushed as fast as possible by detachments of men who had been detailed for that service at Hinckley. Bodies were being found and brought in from all directions. Every effort was made to identify them, but identification was out of the question, unless by some metal article or trinket that was found near or upon the bodies. A strict record was kept of them and they were then turned over to the burial committee at the cemetary under the supervision of F. G. Webber, who did a noble work in this capacity, which from its very nature was one of the most horrible duties that ever devolved upon a human being. The first three days after the fire were very warm and dry, and it was found to be absolutely necessary from a sanitary point of view that the bodies should all be intered at the earliest possible moment, and to this end Mr. Webber staid at his post without rest or sleep for three days and three nights, or until the work had been practically accomplished. After the dead in the immediate neighborhood of the town itself had been intered parties were sent out over the surrounding country to find the remains and bury the victims in the farming districts. They were buried where they

BRINGING THE SURVIVORS TO PINE CITY.

were found, and a board placed with the name of the victim on each grave when there was anything found to make it possible to identify the body. Accurate data as to the interment was also kept and filed with the commissioner.

We will now return to the survivors of Jim Root's train at Skunk Lake who were undergoing sufferings more extreme and more terrible, if possible, than those of their colleagues at Hinckley. After leaving the train and reaching the friendly waters of that mud-hole their sufferings for four hours in that marsh are terrible beyond description. At the first burst of the flame some one shouted "get under the water for your lives." A command which all obeyed, some even submerging themselves entirely for an instant until the worst was past. They had scarcely reached the water, when in a seconds time, the smoke which had been so black and dense that as a survivor said "one could not see his hand held up before his face," seemed to explode and burst into a seething sheet of flame, consuming the gases in the air and igniting everything inflamable, and attended by a crackling and hissing sound truly diabolical. A wall of flame on all sides, seemingly twenty feet high hemmed in the little asylum in which these people had sought safety. After the smoke had cleared away a little the coaches could be seen on the track blazing furiously, and in the course of a

short time the heat from them became so intense
and terrific that the unfortunates were again compelled to immerse themselves entirely in order to
make the heat even endurable. How the women
and children ever survived the terrible ordeal will
always be a mystery, but there were men enough
in the party to keep them drenched with water,
and as some unfortunate became overcome and
swooned there was a clear head and a strong arm
to support and assist them until the terrible period
of heat had passed.

Still it was too hot for them to leave the water
and four hours of mortal agony passed before
they even attempted to do so, and when the time
finally came and they dared leave the lake, they
did so gradually and by degrees retreating first to
the shallow water, then to the mud, then to the
damp ground, and finally high and dry upon the
ground itself. If these people had but known it
there was a much larger body of water on the
other side of the track but a little distance away
where they would have suffered much less if they
had gotten to it. But in the awful moment of
leaving the train nobody thought of it, and perhaps
nobody knew of it and of course it was impossible
to see any distance away. At this time, the men in
the party took a hasty survey of the band to decide
who were the best able to go to Pine City for help.
The lot fell upon three traveling men who hap-

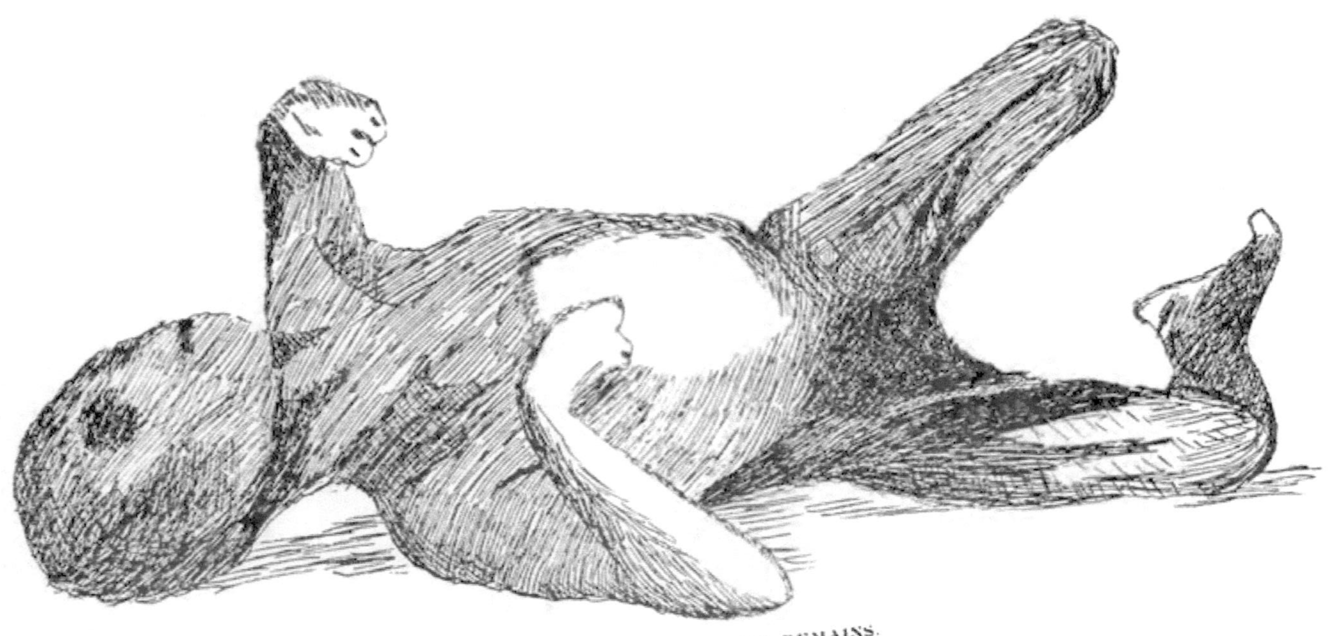

APPEARANCE OF CHARRED REMAINS.

pened to be on board the ill-fated train, Mr. James E. Lobdell of St. Paul, a Mr. Holt of Duluth and a Mr. Anderson of Minneapolis, as being the strongest men physically in the party, and the best able and best fitted for this battle royal with the elements in the shape of a fifteen mile walk over burned ties and amid smoking ruins to a place of safety, and to bring relief to their suffering fellow-men. It was no small undertaking. Fires were still burniug on all sides and the smoke was still thick and the night was very dark, yet these men taking some clothing which had been saved by the convulsive grasp of a traveling salesman, upon, what one might almost call a part of his anatomy, his grip, tore into strips and wrapped it around their feet an ankles so that they were well protected from the burning cinders, etc., and wetting their coats and wrappiug them about their heads, they started their perilous journey to Pine City.

It was indeed an awful and a gruesome task. They wended their way with much difficulty back to where the town had been, through the still burning forests stumbling along, bearly escaping instant death by the fall of a telegraph pole or a giant tamarac as they gave up the ghost to the grim monster, and in the interval between Skunk Lake and Hinckley they counted twenty-nine bodies. Some of these unfortunates had been riding on the platform and overcome by the heat, they had dropped to their death on the tracks below, others were those of the passengers already mentioned who became insane during the flight toward Skunk Lake, and had thrown themselves through the car-windows, and still others were settlers through the country who thought their only safety lay in reaching the town, and they had died upon the track in their attempt to do so. The bridge across the river at Hinckley they did not dare attempt to cross, so they endeavored to find a skiff or something with which they might succeed in crossing the stream, they found nothing that would avail them anything however, and after taking off the burned clothes from their feet and such clothes as would impede their progress they started to wade the stream which is very shallow at this time of the year. On the way across five bodies were discovered, one woman, two men and two children. After six miles of the most awful experiences, and a period covering an hour and forty minutes time they reached the round-house at Hinckley, which was the only vestige that remained, aside from the twisted track itself that would even suggest that this had been the center of a civilized community.

Everything was still as death, and our heroes entered the round-house and threw themselves on the earthern floor of its friendly protection where they remained for about half an hour for they were nearly exhausted, when they once more resumed their journey to Mission Creek first and then to Pine City. They had gone but a short distance from Hinckley when they discovered an abandoned hand car which they appropriated and pushed on to Mission Creek with it. A few miles farther on they met the work train and informed the trainmen of the terrible plight of the passengers of the Duluth Limited at Skunk Lake.

The work train took them back to Pine City where an expedition was immediately organized for the relief of the suffering unfortunates on board Jim Root's train. The news bearers were kindly cared for and given medical assistance, and went to St. Paul by the first special, arriving there about three o'clock in the afternoon or about twenty-four hours after the calamity occurred. Mr. Anderson, one of the three who made this trip which we have just described was himself a loser to the extent of $20,000 which he had with him in the shape of government bonds. which were of course burned with his grip.

CHAPTER IX

SYSTEMATIC RELIEF.

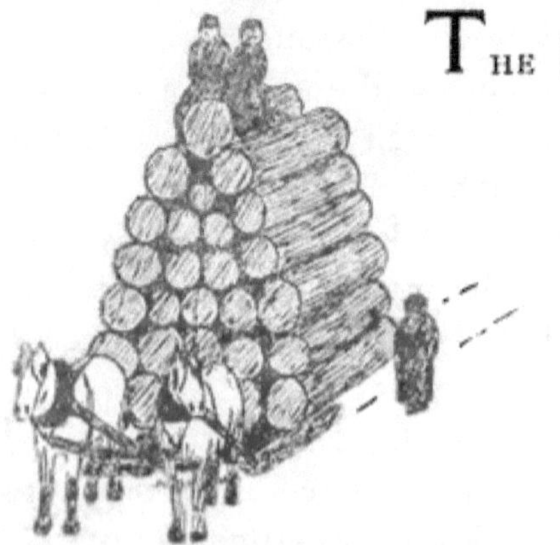

The first train from Saint Paul to Pine City after the fire was a special consisting of one baggage car and one coach besides the engine and ran out on t h e D u l u t h road about 1:25 Sunday morning. It was in no sense a relief train, but was run out in the interest of the road, and conveyed L. S. Miller, assistant general manager, and also the road-master of the Duluth road. At a quarter past eleven on a bright Sunday morning, Tams Bixby, the governor's private secretary, received a telegram from Pine City, stating something in regard to the extent of the fire and asking immediate assistance from St. Paul and her sister city, Minneapolis. They responded nobly, as in the lapse, of the short period of four and a half hours a special train was standing on a side-track at the St. Paul Depot loaded with everything that was deemed necessary and useful, ready to start for the scene of the disaster. Immediately upon receipt of the telegram, a short consultation was held between Governor Nelson, Mr. Bixby and Mr. Harris Richardson of St. Paul and a plan of action was decided on which was put into execution; and in less than fifteen minutes Mr. Bixby was making the telephone wires warm in his endeavor to locate a number of the large wholesalers of the town and gain from them the goods which alone could relieve the sufferers in the burned district. P. H. Kelly and George R. Finch were notified of the situation as was also Capt. W. H. Hart of the National Guard of the State of Minnesota and Capt. Bunker. The Hackett Hardware Co., was also enlisted in the hurried canvas, and by three o'clock in the afternoon a special was standing on a track at the Union Depot in St. Paul and men and wagons were busy loading it with goods of every conceivable description that would be available under such circumstances. There were boxes, crates and barrels, sacks and boxes galore, blankets, frying pans, coffee, pots, knives, forks, plates, tea, coffee, sugar, bacon, beans, flour, corned beef, salt, crackers, and twenty-five hundred

loaves of bread. Everything that could be furnished a stricken people was readily donated and
forwarded as quickly as men could work and steam
could carry it to the scene of the disaster. Mr.
Bixby telegraphed Mr. Hodge, the chairman of
the Pine City Relief Committee inquiring of him
what was needed for the relief of the sufferers.
The reply came with a list of just such things as
had already been furnished with the exception of
one item, "money" a goodly sum of which was
taken up by the committee who accompanied this
first car-load of provisions to the scene. The relief
train left the depot at about four o'clock in the
afternoon, Sunday, Sept. 2nd or just twenty-four
hours from the time the fire broke over Hinckley
with its hurricane of fury. It was accompanied
by a committee of St. Paulites composed of H. D.
Davis, P. H. Kelly, Lane K. Stone, Geo. R. Finch,
Harris Richardson, Jules H. Burwell, D. H. Moon,
Dr. R. H. Wheaton, C. R. Smith, J. G. Donnelly
the undertaker and two assistants, Capt. Bunker,
a detachment of ten volunteers from Company C,
1st Regt. N. G. S. M., under Capt. Montfort and
representatives of the Twin City Press. The Union
Depot in the vicinity of the train presented quite a
lively and peculiar spectacle just before the de-
parture of the train for the relief. The platform
was crowded with spectators who had by some
means or other become aware of the awful calam-

ity which had taken place so near home, and
had gathered here to view the efforts that were
being made to alleviate the suffering of their brothers in the northern pines; and it was a curious
spectacle that presented itself. In one end of the
car were piled stacks of bread clear to the very
ceiling carefully guarded from the dirt by cloths
and papers, while the other end presented a motley array of things edible and useful. The car
was more than full and it was found necessary to
call into service the half of the next car before
all the provisions were taken on board. After
having pulled out from the depot the Relief train
stopped in the lower yard and coupled on a sleep-
er after which the train hastened on its errand of
mercy to its destination. The need of tents had
been anticipated for the shelter of not only the
sufferers but the crowd of curious spectators who
flocked to Pine City by every train on one pretext
or another, some looking for a lost one, some seeking to help anyone and others from mere idle cur-
iosity and this latter class were by no means in
the minority.

Arrangements were immediatly made by Capt.
Hart, Brigadier-Quartermaster, to have the use of
the tents belonging to the State, used by the
National Guard at their annual encampment at
Lake City, at which point the tents still remained.
The commissary at that point at once set to work

to ship the tents, one hundred and ninety in number, to the scene, but for some reason or other the work was delayed so that the tents were not shipped until five o'clock in the afternoon. When they arrived in St. Paul they were immediately switched onto the Duluth track from the Milwaukee road and preparations were immediately made to send them out that night. It was then about eight o'clock in the evening, but word was received that Pine City had prepared a shelter for everyone that night so the train was held until about five o'clock the next morning when it left for the scene with another load of supplies and equipment of helpers.

So much has been said in the past of soulless corporations, that it seems to me no more than right that the railroad companies intimately connected with this disaster should receive the commendation and credit they deserve for the manner in which they handled the affair. Placed as they were under conditions that handicapped them to so great an extent, in the shape of the total demoralization of all communication either postal or telegraphic with the doomed sections and the injury to their road-bed from the burning of bridges, culverts, etc. although they were losers themselves to an enormous extent, they never faltered in their endeavor to succor those who were dependent upon them, but stood ready, eager and willing to offer every assistance in their power to those who were even less

FEEDING THE SURVIVORS AT PINE CITY.

fortunate than they. All supplies were carried free
of cost, not only as soon as the fire had passed,
but as long as anything was still to be sent to the
sufferers, and even at this time six weeks after the
fire has passed they are still carrying the contributions of generous-hearted citizens to their ob-
jective destination.

Too much commendation cannot be given the
Press representatives for their untiring efforts in
giving to the public a most authentic and full account of the terrible conflagration. As it has no
parallel in history so it is a fact, that no occurence
of modern times has quickened the pulse of a nation or in fact the world, as has this fire. It is also a fact that never has a thing of this sort been
more fully or minutely described by the press at
large, and never has the wants of a needy people
been more generously advertised than were those
of the Hinckley fire sufferers at the hands of the
Press of the world, or more especially the press of
the cities of St. Paul, Minneapolis, Duluth an'
West Superior.

At White Bear the relief train stopped and took
on more provisions and a number of Stillwater
gentlemen who had come over to join the rescuing
party, prominint among whom were Judge Neth-
way, H. T. King, Dr. C. W. Merry and Geo. H.
Sullivan.' They immediatley pushed on and at 5:45
were side-tracked at Rush City to make way for

the return of the train which had gone up early in
the day with Assistant General Manager Miller
of the Duluth road on board. Mr. Miller had the
relief train flagged in order to confer with those in
charge of the provisions and give them a better
idea of the extent of the damage and what they
might expect they had to contend with. He told
them to take the stores to Pine City, that they
had a thoroughly organized relief committee there
and that every effort was being made to get the
sufferers to Pine City as soon as possible. One
hundred gallons of milk were taken on at Rush
City. The forest fires could still be seen blazing
here and there as they advanced from Rush City,
exhibiting a pyrotechnic display against the dark-
ening horizon which would set at naught any attempt of man in that direction, and adding much
that was weird and uncanny to the already dreary
and desolate spectacle. They took the advice of
Assistant General Manager Miller, and unloaded
their supplies at Pine City, which was thus made
the distributing point for the burned district.
Upon arriving at Pine City they found a committee of citizens of Pine City with the situation
well in hand, composed of Joseph Hurley, J. F.
Stone, E. A. Hough, H. Berchers and John Y.
Breckenridge. The work train had returned from
its trip up the road and the party on board
reported what was needed most was food, and just

such supplies as the relief train had brought.
After a hurried canvass of the situation and render-
ing what assistance was in its power the relief
train left Pine City for St. Paul at about eleven
o'clock in the evening, leaving behind a number of
the St. Paul committee who were to take an active
part in the relief operations that were to follow in
the next few days. Nothing of interest or importance occurred on the return trip, and the train
reached the St. Paul depot at about half past one
on the morning of the third. After having seen
that the wants of the sufferers were temporarily
relieved, Gov. Nelson, promptly made preparations
for the more serious duty of furnishing the unfortunates with some permanent means of support. A few had a little insurance, but most of
them were left absolutely penniless. In many
cases there was absolutely nothing left of the farm
but the bare land and the mortgage, oft-times the
farm had been consumed, that is to say, the top
soil had been completely burned off, and a sterile
expanse left in its place; but the tenacity of the life
of the mortgage cannot but be remarked upon. At
this time when everything was needed and but
little had been contributed, Gov. Nelson issued a
proclamation to the people of the state requesting
donations and appointing C. A. Pillsbury of
Minneapolis, Kenneth Clark of St. Paul, Charles
H. Graves of Duluth, Mathew G. Norton of Winona.

Hastings H. Hart of St. Paul, a commission in the name of the State to receive money and contributions and forward them to Pine City. Almost simultaneously with this proclamation was one from Mayor Smith of St. Paul to the loyal citizens under his jurisdiction, setting forth the facts in a similar manner, and calling a public meeting to discuss matters and provide ways aud means to furnish the needed supplies and funds. Immediately upon the arrival of the St. Paul Relief Train the relief committee met with the Pine City Relief Committee and organized a general committee in order to better understand and facilitate the work in hand. This committee was composed of Jas. Hurly, chairman; J. F. Stone, J. Y. Breckenridge, E. A. Hough, H. Borchers, of Pine City; Joseph Mannix, Minneapolis; H. E. Quinn, White Bear; J. C. Netheway, Stillwater; J. H. Burwell, Gen. C. S. Bunker, D. H. Moon, Lt. C. R. Smith, P. H. Kelly, Geo. R. Finch, Col. Laird of St. Paul; J. D. Markham, Rush City; and H. T. King, of Stillwater.

A number of other committees were also ap pointed as follows:

COMMITTEE ON CARE OF DEAD.

J. G. Donnelly, H. H. Hart, John E. Dougherty, St. Paul; H. D. Davis, Hinckley; H. G. Perkins, J. W. Hunt, Frank Webber, Father Burke, Dr. E. E. Barnum and John Carmon, of Pine City.

LOCAL EXECUTIVE COMMITTEE.

Jas. Hurley, chairman; E. H. Hough and J. Y. Breckenridge, secretary.

COMMITTEE ON PROVISIONS.

F. A. Hodge, Wm. Smith, Wm. Brouse, John Vaughn, Otto Konalke.

LADIES SUB-COMMITTEE.

Mrs. H. J. Perkins, Mrs. F. A. Hodge, Mrs. Julia Doyce, Mrs. A. Remmington and Mrs. Dale.

A meeting was called and Mr. Jas. Hurley was chosen president and John Y. Breckenridge, secretary. Thus organized the relief work of the committee was taken up in good earnest and much more effective work accomplished in the way of registration of sufferers and distribution of supplies than would have otherwise been possible. All the St. Paul members of the committee were loud in their praises of the most efficient manner in which the Pine City citizens had performed the task which had fallen upon them. Everything that could possibly be done to relieve the suffering had been seen to, and never did a nobler body of men and women undertake a noble work with a greater degree of self-sacrifice and devotion than was exhibited by the good people of Pine City at this time. Never were efforts for their benefit more fully appreciated, and never were a body of unfortunates more truly grateful than were these

fire-sufferers for their much needed succor. After
what they had passed through and had been delivered from, they were grateful indeed to feel that
while they were homeless and alone in one sense
they were still a part of that great body, that
brotherhood which the world calls humanity, and
from her lap of luxury the world at large was
willing and glad to give her portion to aid the
afflicted in their distress, and in the pathetic scenes
that followed the tongue cannot express, and the
pen cannot describe the heartfelt gratitude of the
delivered towards their deliverers.

Active preparations were immediately begun in
both of the Twin Cities for a systematic relief of
the many in need. A meeting of St. Paul citizens
appointed a committee of twenty-one representative business men who were to have complete
charge of all action taken by St. Paul for the relief.
This committee met and appointed an executive
committee to superintend the work. This executive committee consisted of Messrs. E. W. Peet,
chairman; C. W. Hackett, J. J. McCardy, George
Benz, Thomas Cochran, W. J. Footner, and W H
Lightner secretary of committee. Mr. Geo. R.
Finch was later added to the list making eight
members in all.

This committee appointed three sub-committees
to work under its supervision. These committees
consisting of the following gentlemen.

COMMITTEE ON FINANCE.

Gen. Geo. **Bend,** chairman; A. A. Lindeke, E. J. Hodgson, **H. C. McNair and** Richard Gordon

COMMITTEE ON SUPPLIES.

W. L. **Wilson, chairman;** M. L. Hutchins, M. J. O'Connor, Edward Yannish and J. F. **Jackson.**

COMMITTEE ON TRANSPORTATION.

Geo. R . Finch, chairman; Walter A. **Scott** and George Benz.

These committees did some most efficient work in getting **together and** forwarding supplies and funds for the relief of **the** sufferers. **The total** amount of cash **that was collected was** $25,124.40. This was **for the most part turned over to the** State Commission, although, **quite an amount** was expended **by the committee prior to the appointment of the commission by the state; over** $700.00 worth of supplies **having** been sent from St. Paul **to the sufferers** at Cumberland, Wisconsin. This was the first consignment of supplies received at that point **from any** source, and it came in a time of **great need, and** was appreciated by the unfortunates. **Besides the** cash, contributions of all kinds of clothing and furniture were received, which it has been estimated would have been worth in the aggregate at least $10,000. The committee has about completed its labors,

and as soon as the report of its work is audited
they will be placed with the State Historical
Society where they will be held as a matter of
record.

Minneapolis was not one whit behind in the
work of relief which St. Paul had taken up with so
much vigor. A call was issued for a meeting to be
held at the rooms of the Commercial Club in
Minneapolis, which was very well attended by
representative men of all classes.

The meeting was called to order by Mayor
Eustis. C. A. Pillsbury was elected chairman and
Mr. Randolph secretary. Telegrams were read
from the mayor's private secretary, Joseph T.
Mannix, who was on the ground at Pine City and
who stated that Pine City was the basis of opera-
tions, and that the people had enough for imme-
diate needs. After various speeches relative to the
method that should be followed in the work, the
following committee was appointed: C. A. Pillsbury, P. B. Winston, Mayor Eustis, C. M. Loring,
Dr. Hoyt, Geo. Marchand; Mr. Clark, of the
Adams Express Company; Mr. Sullivan, of the
Jobbers' Union; Geo. R. Newell, W. J. Dean, Dr.
Higbee, Senator McMillan, R. V. Squires, A. C.
Haugan, Father Cleary, Rev. J. Falk Gjertsen,
Father Christie, B. F. Nelson. This general committee was afterwards sub-divided into several
smaller committees under different heads in order

to facilitate the work in hand. J. M. Sullivan was
appointed secretary of the committee and P. B.
Winston treasurer.

The sub-executive committee consisted of C. A.
Pillsbury, Mayor Eustis, P. B. Winston and
Harvey Brown.

THE COMMITTEE ON FINANCE.

Nelson Williams, J. T. Wyman, W. J. Dean, Geo.
R. Newell, with F. G. Winston as chairman.

Another committee was appointed to go to Pine
City on the special which was to take up the supplies from Minneapolis as follows:

Messrs Highbee, Marchand, Loring, Winston
and Hoyt.

About $30,000 in cash was raised by this com-
mittee besides a very large amount of clothing,
provisions and other supplies which were sent
from Pine City from time to time. The Minneapolis hospitals received quite a number of those
most seriously injured, and a number of prominent physicians went to Pine City to lend their aid
to the afflicted at that point. It cannot be said of
a single town in the state that they did not do
their part in the great work they were called upon
to accomplish. It was a time when all men were
brothers, all rivalry ceased, and all communities
worked in harmony for the good of the whole.

CHAPTER X

THE RELIEF AT DULUTH.

ST. PAUL and Minneapolis did their share in the work of relief, and at the same time and even previous to the action of the Twin Cities, the citizens of Duluth and West Superior were as actively engaged in caring for the homeless survivors who had been brought to their doors and in making preparations to send other parties to the relief of those who had been less fortunate than their neighbors and were obliged to spend the night in the fire-swept district.

The first intimation to the people of Duluth of the extent of the calamity which had taken place so near to their homes was at 5:55 Saturday afternoon, when Mr. C. M. Phillips, telegraph operator at the general freight office of the St. P. & D. R. R. in Duluth, received the following message from A.

L. Thompson, **telegraph** operator at Miller Station. "The **country is** all burning up, No. **4,** (Root's **train) is burned up. Send Relief."** Mr. Phillips **appreciating the horror of** the situation at once sent **the following telegram to Mr. J. Roper,** conductor **of the freight train** then at Walton **River. "Take engine, caboose and** box cars and go **to relief of** No. **4 passenger, as** Miller reports **they are burned up." Hurry** for God's Sake, sign**ing the** name **of D. H.** Williams, **the St. Paul &** Duluth yardmaster **at Duluth.**

Immediately upon receipt of this urgent appeal, conductor **Roper followed its instructions, and** was on **his way toward the wreck as soon as his** train could **be made up. He ran down to Miller** and brought back **a number of passengers and con**ductor **Sullivan. All the passengers** were so blinded **by ashes and smoke that they could give no definite account of the accident or tell how** it **had** come **to pass. Conductor Sullivan could** see nothing, **and the** pain **in his** eyes **was** so terrible that he became fairly **crazed** and in his agony **it** required **the** attention **of four men to** control him **The crew of Roper's relief train,** though suffering **severely, started back at once to make another at**tempt **to reach the wreck of the limited.** They **proceeded to a point just south of the lower** yards **at Miller where a burned** culvert prevented further **passage. At** this point **they found a** woman in the water close by the track holding a little babe above her head. The two were saved and brought back.

As soon as the news was received at Duluth a special train was made up to go at once to the scene of the disaster, and at 7:05 it left the depot, having on board besides the train crew C. M. Vance, D. H. Williams, Drs Magie, Codding, McCormick and Gilbert and two Duluth newspaper men. The party were fully equipped with provisions, cots, blankets, medical supplies, surgical instruments and everything that they thought could be of use in the relief of the sufferers. Shortly after ten o'clock this train reached Rutledge and at eleven o'clock met Roper's train on its second return from an unsuccessful attempt to reach the wreck. The Duluth party boarded Roper's train, and were run down to the culvert which had blocked his progress twice before, just below Miller, and from that point Williams and the doctors took a hand-car and went down through to Skunk Lake, where the passengers of the limited were found in their terribly exhausted condition.

After a hasty examination as to the real condition of affairs, Dave Williams sent his welcome telegram back to the anxious hearts who waited to hear the worst or the best as his verdict might show it to be. His telegram was as follows:

"Have been to wreck with hand-car." Could only get to Miller with train. Wreck one and a half miles south of Sandstone Junction and is all burned up. "Passengers are all right but exhausted." They are in a marsh. We go with timber to build bridge. Tell everyone all are alive and as well as can be expected. Will arrive in Duluth at 9 A. M.

DAVE WILLIAMS.

At about the same time or shortly after Dave Williams arrived upon the scene with his party, Dr. Barnum's detachment had worked their way through from Pine City with their train of hand-cars, and as the gray of the morning broke what might be termed the St. Paul contingent of the sufferers, about forty in number were loaded on to the hand cars and taken to Pine City, and from thence to St. Paul. The balance were transported to the relief train which had come down from Duluth and taken to that point to be cared for, where they arrived shortly after noon on Sunday. Long before their arrival, the Union Depot was crowded with many hundred people all anxiously waiting for news. Men and women were there hoping for the best, yet fearing that they should receive bad news. When the train finally arrived and it was given out that all were safe, happiness was depicted on every countenance; friends soon found friends, and in an incredibly short space of

time all of the survivors had been temporarily provided for at least.

Early Saturday evening Mayor Lewis, of Duluth,
received a dispatch that 500 people from Hinckley
would arrive at 9 o'clock over the Eastern Minnesota road and would have to be cared for. This
was the first confirmation of the rumor that
Hinckley had burned, and this train was the
Emergency Train, the escape of which from Hinckley has been described in a preceding chapter. The
truth of the telegram was verified at 9:20 when
the train arrived at Duluth with its forlorn cargo
of suffering humanity. A squad of police was at
the depot and kept the crowd back, and Mayor
Lewis spoke to the refugees, saying a few words of
re-assurance, and informing them of what
measures had already been taken for their relief.
They were then taken in charge by the Mayor and
Chief of Police Armstrong, and piloted to the
Ideal and Zenith restaurants and given a square
meal. Lodging was then furnished for the night.
Citizens vieing with one another in alleviating the
distress of the homeless. Many homes of private
citizens were opened and everything that was
available was thrown open for the use of the
sufferers. Twenty-five families were accommoda-
ted in the Wolf Block. The Columbia Hotel, the
Duluth Hotel, the Armory, the Howard Block and
the Union Depot, all figured conspicuously in the

shelter of the unfortunates both at this time and until they could be otherwise provided for.

After having given temporary relief to the sufferers on the evening of their arrival the generous-hearted people of Duluth turned out Sunday morning as one man, whose only thought and action was to care for those whom fate had placed in a position where they could not take care of themselves. The following proclamation was issued in the Duluth papers Sunday morning, and under the circumstances it would seem as if such a clear concise, yet earnest and heartfelt appeal could not fail to elicit the hearty support it received.

PROCLAMATION!

Mayor's Office. }
Duluth, Sept. 2, '94. }

A meeting of the business men and citizens of Duluth will be held at the council chamber in the city hall at 11 o'clock this morning for the purpose of appointing a relief committee to provide ways and means for the care of the people who have been left destitute and homeless by the disastrous fire, which has burned so many flourishing neighboring towns. Hundreds ot men, women and children were brought to the city last night and are in the armory and in lodging houses down town, who have lost their all and are scantily clothed. We must provide food and clothes for them at once. The occasion demands immediate action and I feel assured that there will be a hearty response to this call.

RAY T. LEWIS,
Mayor.

In response to the mayor's proclamation at eleven o'clock on that Sunday morning the City Hall at Duluth was filled to over-flowing with many of Duluth's most prominent and best citizens. The meeting was called to order by Mayor Lewis, and in a very short time an organization for systematic relief was effected, after which Mayor Lewis as chairman appointed the following committees who immediately entered upon the discharge of their several duties, and of whose efficient service too much commendation cannot be given.

Under the head of a general relief committee whose duty should be to superintend and oversee the whole work. Mr. Lewis appointed John T. Hale, chairman; E. C. 'Gridley, A. C. Batchelor, J. B. Geggie, C. D. Autremont, Bishop McGolrick and Ward Ames. Mrs. Miller, President of the Ladies' Relief Society, and E. M. Bangs, Superintendent of the Associated Charities of Duluth. This general committee met and organized for more definite work and appointed the following committees:

COMMITTEE ON TRANSPORTATION.

W. Buchanan, E. C. Holliday and J. M. Smith.

COMMITTEE ON FINANCE.

A. B. Chapin, Wm. Craig and Otto Hartman.

COMMITTEE ON LUMBER AND GENERAL SUPPLIES.

Bishop McGolrick, chairman; Mr. J. G. Howard, Mr. H. B. Moore, Mr. W. T. Bailey, Mr. G. A. Leland, Mr. W. B. Weller, Mr. H. C. Shephard.

COMMITTEE ON ROOMS, QUARTERS AND COMMISSARY.

Mr. J. B. Geggie, Mr. A. E. Batchelor, Mrs. E. M. Bangs.

COMMITTEE ON INFORMATION, IDENTIFICATION AND ADOPTION.

Mr. C. F. Johnson, Mr. F. Davis, Mr. A. P. Cook, Mrs. E. M. Bangs.

AUDITING COMMITTEE.

C. R. Haines, chairman; J. C. Hunter and J. Megins.

COMMITTEE ON INSURANCE LOANS.

Mr. R. A. Tanssig and Mr. W. E. Wright.

COMMITTEE ON CLOTHING.

Ladies' Relief Society.

COMMITTEE ON WIDOWS AND ORPHANS.

Hon. J. T. Hale, Hon. C. D. Autremont and Mrs. E. M. Bangs.

At the suggestion of the State Commission Mr. John G. Howard, of Duluth, was sent to the burned district to take charge of the building up of those places. Mr. N. J. Miller was appointed to assist him. The following extract from the pen of Mrs. E. M. Bangs, who acted as secretary of the Duluth General Relief Committee will convey a more accurate idea of the condition of things in general in Duluth than I could possibly hope to do.

"We estimate that we had fully fifteen hundred people to care for the first two weeks or more.

Private houses, churches, the Bethel, the Armory,
and Odd Fellows' Hall, were all thrown open for
any use the committees might make of them. The
Maternity Hospital and Duluth Home were also
used, as well as quarters in the Berkelman Block.
In all of these places the work was quickly and
effectually done, the churches adjourning their
services on Sunday morning to prepare their com-
modious church parlors and Sunday School rooms
into comfortable quarters for the crowds of fire
sufferers, pouring utterly destitute into our city.
It would be impossible to enumerate in detail, or
mention individual excellence in work where so
many did their uttermost. Suffice it to say that
the whole town rose as one person to offer and
give the best they could afford, were it time,
strength, money, clothing, food, or kind words
and helpful deeds of sympathy.

The total receipts of the Duluth Citizens Relief
Committee for the forest fire sufferers in cash,
lumber, provisions, clothing, etc., is up to date a
little more than $20,000, and the committee have
disbursed up this time in cash about fifteen thousand dollars, besides thousands of articles of wear-
ing apparel to the needy men, women and children
composing the unfortunate throng of refugees so
suddenly thrown upon our bounty.

Too much praise cannot be given for the able
manner in which Mr. Gridley conducted the work

of the "Citizens Central Relief Committee" during all this trying time. Hon. J. T. Hale had been appointed chairman by the mayor, but owing to recent illness was obliged to decline. As soon as Mr. Gridley learned of his appointment, he immediately organized the committee work in the most systematic manner. A very large and spacious room in the *Herald* building was secured, and in less than half an hour the following committees were at work at tables on either side of the room, with printed cards on the walls telling what each committee was. The room looked like a well organized bank. There these faithful committees worked every day, and many times way into the night for six weeks or more during the most intense heat and trying conditions, most of them giving their time to the neglect of their own business interest. No one can imagine unless one went through it what a tax on ones nervous strength this was. Not once was Mr. Gridley unequal to any emergency which arose, and with the utmost courtesy and kindness treated all who came under his immediate care, answering and deciding in the same spirit all the difficult questions, and deciding with great promptness, and clear and fair-mindedness all the varied problems which arose constantly before him.

The Local Relief Committee are up to this date, Nov. 16, 1894, still caring for about two hundred

fire sufferers, who will doubtless be more or less
helpless through the winter. At a meeting of the
Executive Committee Nov. 15, it was voted to
give each family in our care a Thanksgiving
Dinner of the old, time honored kind."

Mr. W. B. Weller

Mrs. E. M. Bangs.

Committee on · report of Duluth work for fire
sufferers.

*   *   *   *

Another relief train was sent out Sunday afternoon to Miller or Sandstone Junction, and search-
ing parties organized to go to Sandstone on the
Eastern Minnesota. Here were found the remains
of thirty bodies all burned beyond human sem-
blance. They had all fallen within 100 feet of
their homes, and lay in attitudes horribly portray-
ing the agonies of their last struggle. Some lay
with their fleshless arms outstretched as if
beseeching aid from a power that is higher than
us, others were found clutching the earth beneath
them. Children were found close to their mothers—
oft-times the mothers own body partially sheltered
that of the child, showing the filial affection pre-
dominant even to death. Two hundred and forty-
seven of the survivors were conducted across the
country three miles to Miller, from whence they
were taken to Duluth. Their eyes were affected by
the heat and smoke that for the most part it was

found necessary to lead them to the train as a person would lead a blind man.

During Sunday night the first relief train went down over the Eastern Minnesota. Owing to burned bridges it was found to be impossible to get beyond Partridge, eight miles above Sandstone; and from that point hand cars were taken, and each succeeding train brought in some survivors from Sandstone, or Hellgate, a sand-stone quarry near by. It were useless to attempt to enumerate all that was done and all the methods employed by the good people of Duluth for their afflicted neighbors. Train after train was sent out on its errand of mercy and returned laden with additional responsibilities for Duluth citizens to assume. Duluth was the first on the scene, the first to start a relief fund, and foremost in every way in doing all in her power for the fire sufferers.

Others may have done all in their power for the sufferers, but it is certainly a fact that it lay in the power of the good people of Duluth to accomplish more for their alleviation than was possible for those at a greater distance from the scene of the disaster. The care of fifteen hundred destitute people having in most cases not even clothes on their backs, brought from a state of prosperity to one of abject poverty, almost in less time than it takes to tell it, discouraged and sorrowing for ones loved and lost, is no small undertaking. Others at a distance might express their sympathy by the pratical prosaic method of a check that was drawn on a bank in the same way that hundreds of others had been, and once drawn would be sent and then forgotten, but it required sympathy of a different sort to sooth the sorrows of the child left utterly alone in the world, without money, without family and without friends.

A few dollars in cold cash could not relieve the widow of the thought that upon her frail form rested the burden of providing and caring for her little brood, which had up to this time been sheltered as well by a father's love and a father's blessing. Coming in contact day after day with scenes like these, feeling obliged to assist when one's own physical had been taxed to its very utmost, and almost cried out in protest against such wanton disregard of the laws of nature, feeling the responsibility that rested upon them, the general committee of Duluth have accomplished the work laid at their door in a manner that was wonderfully prompt, efficient and effective, and for their good work deserve and should receive the heartfelt thanks of a grateful nation.

CHAPTER XI.

THE excitement attendant upon the news of Hinckley's loss having slightly abated, the leaders appreciated the extent of the calamity and the magnitude of the work in hand, and the clear-headed saw it was absolutely necessay to systematize the work a great deal in order to insure the proper and equitable distribution of the funds and materials. To this end registration and death blanks were printed and the the work of procuring some definite information as to who were to be providedfor and what was necessary for them, or in other words what they needed. In order to register, a refugee was called upon to give his name, his birth place and also the name and birth-place of his wife and children, his residence, and how long he had lived in Minnesota. If a farmer the location of his land and the conditions upon which he held it. That is to say a great part of this section was railroad land which had at one time been held by one of the rail road companies and was still held either by them or one of the large land companies, of which there were several. If a man desired to buy a piece of land he would pick it out and would be given what is known as a land contract upon it, that is a contract of sale of a certain piece of property for so much money, to be paid under certain conditions. usually so much a year, and agreeing to give a deed to the property when a certain amount of money had been paid, and take a mortgage for the balance. Thus giving the settler immediate possession of the property and enabling him to buy it in such a way that he would be able to pay for it. A great majority of the farmers in this section had their payments to meet on these contracts and one of the first duties that devolved upon the commission was to interview these Land Companies and secure such extension of the payments as would enable the settlers to get a start again before being obliged to give up what they had already invested for non-payment for their land. A great many mortgages were also extended in the same way. Another thing the commission sought to know was how much insurance, if any, the register carried. The insurance companies, however, seemed to anticipate something of this nature; they were loth to take risks in this section, and for this reason the rates were high and the amount of insurance comparatively small. The idea of the settler seeming to be that he would carry just enough insuranee to pay his debts and let it go at that.

Next came the question what property he had left and its value. Then the address of friends and their ability to furnish aid or work for the refugees.

After the foregoing came the all important question of what the applicant needed, whether he wanted to go back on his farm or to his home, and if not, where he wanted to go. In one particular at least all the sufferers are alike, they all needed clothes and food. As soon as they were registered they were given tickets to the store-keeper of the commission who would fit them out for clothes, it being the idea to give them a fair outfit not only of outer garments but under-clothing as well, at least two suits of underwear being furnished each person. They were also given a ticket which would give them a supply of food.

It was not in any instance the intention of the commission to place any one in a better position after the fire than he had been before, and the question was to determine how much each was capable of doing for himself and how much would be necessary in order to place them in a position that would make them self-supporting during the coming winter. At the outset the commission was greatly handicapped in its workings in that, it was almost entirely lacking of facilities of transportation and of buildings in which to work. There was nothing left at Hinckley, not even a spear of hay for the cattle, and it is a fact that the animals who did succeed in escaping the fire nearly starved before provisions could be brought to them.

The blank that was filled out for registration of the dead required similar information as to their past as was procured of the living. To this was added where they were found; by whom identified and how; where they were buried; valuables on the person; in whose custody the valuables were left and the name and address of any living friends. After the survivors had been registered and received their guarantee of food and clothing the commission took up each individual case, and investigated their wants thoroughly. While no exact rule was laid down for the distribution of the funds, their approximate distribution amounted to about $25.00 per member of the family, but this varied more or less as the case might be, and a fair distribution might demand. Single men and women were allowed an outfit of clothes and $15.00 in money, and were given either work or transportation. A man and his wife and baby would receive $60.00, and if it were three children would receive $100.00 besides food and clothing. Farmers were furnished a few plain tools and in cases where the land contract had been extended or the mortgage renewed a small, neat and compact house was given him, or if he wished to cut the charred trees and build himself a log house such as many of them had occupied, the means were furnished him whereby it might be done.

Besides furnishing the house itself the commission supplied a few pieces of furniture such as were necessary for house-keeping, which although plain were comfortable and durable, and also crockery and bedding sufficient to supply their immediate wants. Mr. Hart, of the State Commission, tells me that in some cases where there were young children in the family the commission furnished them a cow, though this was not possible except in cases where it was thought to be especially needed. It had been hoped that they would be able to give every farmer at least one cow, and perhaps a wagon, but that is now out of the question, as the funds of the commission have already been spent.

The total amount of money received by the State Commission for the sufferers from all sources up to this time, Nov. 22, 1894, is $91,000. Of this amount the citizens of St. Paul contributed $32,000, Minneapolis, $30,000. The balance was received from various points all over the state. The Governor's proclamation having called forth a very general action on the part of all the communities in the state, and meetings were held, local committees appointed, collection made and forwarded to Mr. Clark, treasurer of the commission. While the following is not a complete list of towns from which contributions were received it is a list of all the more important points. Duluth, Winona, West Superior, Mankato, St. Peter, Le Seuer, Red Wing, Lake City, Spring Valley, Fargo, Moorhead, Grand Forks, Glynden, Crookston, Litchfield, Fergus Falls, Redwood Falls, Montevido, New Ulm, Pipestone, Henderson, Heron Lake, Benson, Wadena, Elbow Lake, Chaska, Rochester, Preston, Sauk Rapids, Mora, Brainerd, Aitken, Benson, Morris, Glenwood, Sauk Centre, Alexandria, Detroit City, Park Rapids, Ortonville, Marshall, Howard Falls, Windom, Luverne, Albert Lea, Waseca, Cannon Falls, Northfield, Faribault, Center City, Brown's Valley, Graceville and Renville.

It will be seen by the above that the State of Minnesota responded nobly to the call for aid for her suffering citizens, and if this list were complete it would include every hamlet within the jurisdiction of the state. All responded with alacrity and gave that which they could spare best, were it money, clothes, or provisions, and the railroad companies

without any exception gave free transportation on
their lines for all supplies destined to relieve the
distress of the fire victims. Beside the cash relief
fund mentioned an immense amount of clothing,
household supplies and provisions were contributed
to the sufferers. Methods of all sorts were enlisted
in the work of raising funds, and numbers of enter-
tainments were given, the proceeds of which were
dedicated to the fire.

Although the newspapers all over the country
published a great many reports of the fire, and a
sympathetic nation deplored the condition of the
Hinckley fire sufferers, comparatively few contributions were received from points outside of the
State of Minnesota. Chicago contributed about
$1,000. A number of the eastern states perhaps
as much more, but ninety per cent at least of the
money received by the commission was donated by
Minnesota citizens. There may have been individual contributions from outside parties to the
sufferers themselves of which the commission has
no means of knowing, but aside from that, Minnesota contributed the lion's share.

Quite an amount of money had also been ex-
pended by the local committee of St. Paul, Minneapolis and Duluth, prior to the assumption of the
charge of affairs by the commission appointed by
the Governor. The St. Paul & Duluth road gave
at least $10,000 in freight and transportation,

and the Great Northern must have contributed nearly as large an amount in the same way.

At the time the commission took hold of the work they had been led to believe that about 1,500 people would come under their charge, but registration showed a census of residents of 2,400 people. They have built for these people 300 houses, using over 2,000,000 feet of lumber in the construction of the same. They have furnished 450 families with complete outfits of furniture, household goods and cooking utensils, as well as clothing, boots and shoes, and all the numerous small articles which are necessary for the comfort and convenience of the household. They have furnished them with provisions, and will continue to do so until such time as they are able to take care of themselves. They have now on hand distributed among the various families provisions sufficient to supply them for a period of three months, and Mr. Hart estimates that at least $20,000 more will be required to supply all that will be needed before spring.

The people of the burned districts as a rule were satisfied with the distribution of the funds as accomplished by the commission. Of course, there were some who felt very much dissatisfied with themselves, and everyone else because it was not in the power of the commission to give them enough to place them in a position, equal in all

respects to the one they occupied before the fire.
They would have been dissatisfied in any event,
and the commission has certainly done all in its
power to insure a speedy and equitable distribution of the supplies at their disposal, and should
receive not the censure, but the gratitude and commendation of the entire state, as well as the
afflicted Hinckleyites for the efficient manner in
which they have served the commonwealth in this
time of distress. They were all men of business,
yet they devoted their time and energy to this
work without a thought of renumeration, and
would not have accepted it had it been offered
them. The Rev. H. H. Hart, secretary of the State
Board of Corrections and Charities, superintended
the entire work of the commission, and for two
months time put body and soul into the task. He
seemed to be almost omni-present as his duties led
him from one place to another, either to learn what
was needed most and how much could be allowed,
or how it could best be furnished.

Mr. J. G. Howard, of Duluth, also rendered most
efficient service in overseeing and providing for
the erection of all of the houses of the commission.
He also worked without renumeration. In a con-
versation with Rev. H. H. Hart, relative to the
fire, he said: "The vigor with which some of these
people have taken up the work of their own relief
is certainly very gratifying to those who have at-

IN THE TEMPORARY HOSPITAL AT PINE CITY.

tempted to aid them, and alleviate their condition. As a class they are hopeful and earnest in the work of re-building their homes. One young man I know of, who lost everything, has done an amount of work that is little short of miraculous since the fire. Another poor fellow whose hands were so terribly burned that he has not, even yet, recovered the use of them was seen a day or two ago driving a team with both hands bandaged and bundled in lint and cloth. Some, however, seem to be discouraged, and these for the most part are those who for some reason were obliged to wait and idle away their time for the first few days after the fire. Thus giving them time to think and brood over their misfortune.

This might have been averted had we been able to furnish them something to busy their hands with as soon as the fire had passed. The commission established a depot at Hinckley and also one at Sandstone, and a warehouse was built at Hinckley for the purpose of holding the stores received for the sufferers. The Hinckley Depot has been abolished so far as the office is concerned, and the one at Sandstone will be in the course of a short time, although the commission will keep in touch with its proteges through its representative Mr. Geo. D. Holt, of Mlnneapolis, who will make bi-weekly visits to the sufferers and see to it that all are kept from want. The approach of winter is looked upon with comparatively little apprehension, as most of the families are able to take care of themselves with the assistance they have already received, and as logging has already been undertaken very extensively by the lumbermen, who will be obliged to cut all the standing pine in the district burned over this winter, in order to preserve it from the ravages of the worms, who will make their appearance next spring and summer, and there will be work enough to employ all the men who care to work in the woods.

One lumberman alone is now employing 1,200 men within eight miles of Hinckley, and expects to bank 150,000,000 feet of logs this year, when as a rule he cuts about 15,000,000 feet per annum. At Sandstone the quarry is employing 100 men at the present time, and the Great Northern Railway is making extensive improvements and making Sandstone a division point, employing over a hundred men now, and expecting to employ a great many more shortly. At the present time there is no individual in the whole fire district that is suffering in any way that could be relieved by the commission.

CHAPTER XII.

MR. JAMES ROOT, the heroic engineer of the Duluth limited which ran back and was burned at Skunk Lake, gave the author the following as his story of the terrible ride for life on the first day of September, 1894. Mr. Root is a modest appearing man, a little above the medium height, with an open, honest face, and a general bearing that would convey to a careful observer the impression that he was not a mere carpet knight, but one of sterling worth who could and would understand and do without flinching any duty that might be placed upon him. He talked freely, yet not boastfully of his experience and told his story as follows:

"When we left Duluth we were on time, and I think when we got to Carlton we were not more than ten minutes late, at all events, we were practically on time when we got to the top of the hill at Hinckley. We had been running through smoke that was so thick and dense that they had lighted the lamps in the coaches, and I had the cab lamp lit, but as we reached the hill the smoke cleared and it was broad day light again and we blew the lights out. Then I saw the people coming from both sides of the track and across the bridge, and I said to the fireman, "There must be something wrong at Hinckley," and I applied the air and stopped, seeing so many people on the bridge I knew we couldn't go over it anyway. Just then an old woman and her two daughters came along and I asked them what the trouble was down there. They were so excited they couldn't tell me anything, but kept saying, "For God's sake will you save us," and that was all that I could get out of them. Then the people kept on coming and getting into the cars on both sides until Mr. Bartlett and his wife came along, and I asked them what the trouble was, he says: "Jim, "everybody is burned out and everything is burning at Hinckley." I asked him if the depot was on fire and he said that it was, and the tank-house and the bridge. I told them to hurry and get onto the train for I was going to run back to Skunk Lake

ENGINEER JAMES ROOT.

I then saw the conductor and told him what I was going to do and for him to keep a look-ont for the passengers until we got there. I then climbed onto the engine again, and just as I did so everything seemed to let go; the wind raised; there seemed to be an explosion, and in an instant the whole train, even to the ties under the engine were ignited, all in less time than a man could snap his finger. I had hardly taken my seat when the glass in the cab window at my side, a heavy plate, I saw bend toward me and burst. It was carried to the top of the cab over my head, and as it came down struck me on the left side of the face and head cutting   several quite severe gashes, although at the time I had no idea that I had been hurt at all. I knew I was bleeding a little, but didn't know anything of the cut in my neck from which I suffered so much from loss of blood. McGowan said afterwards that he noticed it, and I asked him why he didn't speak about it as had I known of it I would have put a handkerchief or a bit of waste in it and stopped the flow. He said he didn't think it was anything serious. As I got into the cut at the top of big Hinckley Hill I heard somebody calling, and it proved to be three men who were coming toward the train. I applied the air first thinking of taking them on, but a second thought told me it would not do to stop in that cut as the fire would surely burn a hole in the hose and set us there, so I released the air and we pulled out. Two of these men caught onto the pilot of the engine as we went by, one of them remained there a short time, and then fell off and was burned to death, the other one went through all right and is still alive. That is the last I recollect until we reached what we call Little Hinckley Hill. I was then lying on the deck of the engine with one foot on the quadron and one on the fire-box door. I was all alone in the cab. My engine had slackened her speed and was going very slow. I looked up at the gauge and saw that I had ninety pounds of steam I then pulled myself up and opened the throttle and sat on the seat again. Then the fireman showed himself out of the tank. He was down in the water wholly in the tank. I had commenced to get dizzy again, and was leaning forward, and he reached out his hand to catch me, and as he did so some water from his sleeve touched my face. It was so good, so reviving that I said at once, "For God's sake give me some more of that." He then threw a little more on me, and I told him to draw a pail of water from the tank. He did so, and we both thrust our hands into the water. I said to him, "I believe the back of my hands are cooked, I darsn't rub them," and he said "mine are just the same." My hands were paining me a great deal, and were swollen to twice their normal size when he drew the water, and when I thrust

them into the water it seemed to relieve the pain
entirely, and seemed to revive me very much. I
felt ninety per cent better immediately. I told
Jack to put on some more coal and he threw on
two more shovels full. About the time he had
finished doing that I saw some water in the ditch
at the side of the track and I knew we must have
reached Skunk Lake, as there wasn't a drop of
water within fifteen miles but that, so I applied the
air and stopped her. I found I had stopped right
upon the bridge, so I threw the reverse lever to a
forward motion and pulled ahead a car length or
two. I then fell prone on the deck of the engine.
Jack wanted to help me, but I told him I was all
right and for him to go and get the passengers out
and into the water. He said I would burn to
death there. I told him to never mind me but to go
and get the passengers off and then he could come
back after me. So he did so, and in a few minutes
he came back and he and another man assisted me
off of the engine. As soon as I struck the ground
I rolled into the water and laid there for three
hours, and all of the passengers of the train were
laying or sitting in the water aronnd us, men, women and children. While I was lying there in the
water I seemed to lose the use and feeling of the
lower part of my body. From my hips down to
my feet I had no feeling whatever, so I pulled myself up on the dry ground with my arms and laid

there for about an hour when the feeling all came back to me again, and I commenced to chill. I said to McGowan, "I must get back onto that engine where its warm for I'm chilling to death." He said I couldn't live on there for the coal was all burning, and the cab was all afire. I told him I was going there anyway, so he assisted me back onto the engine. I laid there on the deck a short time and the feeling all came back to me, and I felt pretty well only very weak. While I laid there in the water exhausted, I asked Jack to run back and see if he could put out the fire and save any of the coaches, or if we could cut out any of them. He said it was out of the question, he could do nothing with them so he sat down in the water beside me. When I had gotten back onto the engine again, I asked him if he could put out the fire on the tank, and told him if he couldn't to pull the pin between the tank and the engine and unhook the safety chains, and we would run her ahead out of the way of the fire. He pulled the pin and we ran her ahead about ten feet, away from the tank and let her stand there until she died. The entire train tank and everything burned right up, everything that was of burnable material. Since the matter has passed I have heard certain ones who should be in a position to know better express some words of censure toward the officers of the road for allowing us to run into such a death trap.

FIREMAN JOHN McGOWAN.

saying they should have notified us before, and I
want to set that matter right. Under the circumstances no living man could have foretold what was
in store for us, and all the way down from Carlton
to Hinckley there was nothing to alarm us in any
way other than the smoke which was thick and
dense as I have already stated, but there was no
blaze, there was absolutely no fire to be seen
until that explosion occurred which burst in my
cab window, and seemed to ignite everything
inflamable all in an instant. The first intimation
that I had that anything unusual had ocurred
or was about to occur was when I saw the people
running to meet me at Hinckley. We have had
to run through smoke time and time again every
year. There have always been more or less
forest fires, and as I came out of the smoke at the
top of the hill I thought we had passed it and
everything would be clear sailing. I wish to
say again in justice to the officials that there was
nothing to warrant them in holding my train, nor
is anyone to blame for the occurrence. It could not
have been avoided, and I do not wish to see anyone
censured for something which is not justice. The
first relief party that reached us was that of Dave
Williams, and his crew that came down from the
north on hand-cars. I thought first that I would
go back to Duluth with them, but on reaching the
hand-car I found that I could not sit up, and know-

ing that I would take up so much room that it would keep back two or three others, I made my way back to the engine and told them I would wait. About an hour later the hand-cars came up from the south under conductor Buckley. They had four hand-cars and two push cars, and all the section men that they had picked up from Wyoming all the way down the road. They loaded the weaker ones, myself among them on the cars, and the balance walked to Hinckley. I rode on one of the push cars and Mrs. E. W. Sanders who was on the train supported my head and helped me through. I wish to say a word of Mrs. Sanders. She was never a very strong woman, yet through this whole ordeal she exhibited the greatest fortitude, and I verily believe that when we were found by the relief train she was the clearest witted one in the whole party. While I lay on the engine a Mr. Anderson from Minneapolis came to me and did all that he could to relieve me in every way, wetting cloths and holding them over my eyes, and using every means in his power to ameliorate my condition. When we reached Hinckley on the hand-cars we found a train waiting to take us to Pine City, and then of course we came right on down. I, of course, stopped off at White Bear, at my home, and went to bed and to sleep as I was completely exhausted. I awoke Monday morning however, feeling as well as could be expected. My eyes did not trouble me to amount to anything, and I was not burned badly anywhere. My hands which had been badly swollen did not prove to be really burned at all, and two days after the fire I was none the worse for wear.

Jas Root

Questioned about his past life and his career as a railroad man, Mr. Root said: "I was born in Greenbush, New York in 1843. I commenced my railroading on the Hudson River road in 1857, under Mr. Tousey, who is now General Manager of the New York Central and Hudson River System. I railroaded there until 1860, when I went to La Porte, Indiana, and went to work on the Michigan Southern & Northern Indiana road. I railroaded there about a year and then enlisted as a minute-man to defend the State of Indiana at the time Morgan made his raid through Indiana and Ohio. I was mustered out again after Morgan got back into Kentucky. The regiment I belonged to volunteered to defend the State of Ohio, they not yet having organized a regiment, and drive Morgan back into Kentucky from Ohio. After that I went south and worked on the Louisville & Nashville road with headquarters at Bowling Green. I remained on that road for about seventeen months as engineer and conductor of a work train. The guerillas got after me so I left and went into the employ of the government, and was sent to the front at Knoxville, Tennessee. When Sherman made his great march to the sea, I started with him and we went to a point called Strawberry Plains, but returned and started out again towards Atlanta. I was the engineer on the advance train with him and went with him to a point about sixteen miles north of Atlanta where he met his first actual opposition. I then went back to Chattanooga and got a hospital train and went back with that after the prisoners at Andersonville. We went through the prison and brought all the sick and wounded back to Chattanooga. I remained with the government until 1865, the close of the war. I then came to Hastings, Minnesota, to visit an uncle I had there, and remained there that winter, and the next spring went to Stillwater, Minnesota. At Stillwater I went to work in a lumber mill for Mr. John Atley, and worked with him for about a year and a half. I then put in a winter in the woods, and that spring the St. Paul & Duluth road was building and I made an application for a position as engineer, and in 1870 went to work for the St. Paul & Duluth road at Duluth as engine dispatcher. In 1871 I took an engine out on the road and have served the St. Paul & Duluth Company in that capacity ever since. Of course I have met with a few minor accidents, but nothing of any great importance, and nothing that called out any censure on my part. I married Miss E. M. Fox while I was at work in Stillwater in 1869.

JIM ROOT'S RIDE.

FRANKLYN W. LEE.

When the angel blows his trumpet and the firmanent unrolls.
And the voice of God is calling all the many scattered souls,
There's a man who'll lead a phalanx up the jewelled golden
      street
To a corner they have saved for him beside the mercy seat;
For the angels hate a coward and they love a gritty man
And they know Jim Root's a hero on the strictly gritty plan.

It was early in September, and the earth was just as dry
As a lump of punk and hotter than an upper Congo sky.
There had been no rain since April and it needed but a match,
To engulf the northern district, set it burning like a thatch;
And the people did not wonder when the smoke began to rise
Till a pall hung low and darkly, shutting out the summer
      skies.

Jim was running on the Limited, and when he left Duluth
There were stories of the dangers which seemed only partial
      truth,
But the hand that held the throttle was a hardy one and true

And though hell was on his orders, Jim was bound to take her
      through.
He controlled the lives of many and he knew that all his nerve
Would be needed when he headed for the hades round the curve.

They had made the run to Miller ere the breeze began to scorch
Ere the people saw the waving of that mighty, flaming torch
"But I'll run her through to Hinckley," thought the little
      engineer,
"Where I'll wire in for orders—it is not too far from here;"
And he yelled to Jack McGowan, who was on the other side,
"Crowd the coal and keep her going, for I mean to let her
      slide!"

All the horrors told by Dante, all the pictures by Dore
Are imperfectly suggestive of that blazing right of way
For the universe seemed flaming and the air would fairly
      seethe
Till the people in the coaches found it difficult to breathe,
While the entrance into Hinckley seemed the inner gate of
      hell,
With the devil's imps disporting on the pine trees as they fell.

To have passed beyond the station would have meant the
      death of all;
To have fooled around for orders from some fellow in St. Paul
Would have been the height of folly, and when people who had
      ran
For the train were safely sheltered from the fiend the flight
      began,
And, reversing, Jim moved backward through the awful, blazing
      rain
To a place where he could harbor all the people on the train.

There were flames above, around them, underneath—no hand
      could paint

All the terrors of that moment, which made strong men droop
        and faint.
Every car was like an oven; coaches blistered in the heat;
Panes of glass began to shrivel. and, to make the hour com-
        plete,
Tongues of flames crept through the windows as the train be-
        gan to burn
And a strange and deathlike whiteness crept o'er faces drawn
        and stern.

But Jim Root was on the engine and had naught to bar the
        flame,
Though his hand was on the throttle and he stuck there just
        the same.
As he backed her through the horror. with Skuuk lake six miles
        away,
He had little hope of living to recall that fearful day;
But the engineer was plucky, and with Jack McGowan there
He was good for any duty, for he had a life to spare.

When his hand began to blister, why, the other one was strong,
And when both were singed and broiling they did duty right
        along;
When his overalls were smoking, there was hardy, faithful
        Jack,
Who was standing with a bucket pouring water down his
        back.
Once or twice Jim almost fainted, once or twice fell off his
        seat,
But he rallied like a hero as he fought away the heat.

And he saved a train of people, just for common duty's sake—
Held the throttle, cool and gritty, till they reached the little
        lake,
Till the hundreds went in safety from the charred ill-fated
        train,

And he never gave a whimper in his agony of pain,
Never murmured—no, not even when his fearful ride was o'er
And he sank, all burned and nerveless, on the blackened, burn-
        ing floor.
They will tell you of the heroes who left no good deed undone;
They will say that all the honor should not go to merely one,
But whatever men accomplished for the grateful ones to tell,
When in future years they speak of all the horrors of that hell.

It was Jim, who, sticking bravely in the glaring face of death,
Saved three hundred human beings from the all destroying
        breath.

When the day of judgment cometh and the firmament unrolls,
And the voice of God is calling all the many scattered souls,
There's a man who'll lead a phalanx up the jewelled, golden
        street,
To a corner they have saved for him beside the mercy seat;
For the angels hate a coward, and they love a gritty man,
And they know that Jim's a hero on the strictly gritty plan.

CHAPTER XIII.

EXPERIENCES OF HON. C. D. O'BRIEN
AND OTHERS.

Tʜᴇ Hon. C. D. O'Brien, who was one of the passengers on the Duluth limited gives the following graphic account of the affair as he saw it. He was accompanied by his son Richard, and by his brother, Dr. Harry J. O'Brien. Mr. O'Brien says: "We left Duluth on the St. Paul limited train for St. Paul at 1:55 on the afternoon of September 1st. It had been smoky throughout the northern forests and over Lake Superior for a long period, and as we left Duluth the wind increased strongly from the southwest and smoke rolled down in such quantities that the city of Superior across the bay was no longer visible. We expected that on reaching the top of the hill near Thompson station to get out of the smoke, bnt on arriving at that point the smoke was still in great clouds on both sides of the road, partially obscuring the sun. There were some fires burning between the St. Louis river and the line of road between Thompson and Duluth, but they were not near enough to the track or of sufficient size to create any apprehension. After leaving Thompson the next stop was Hinckley, the point which we never reached, but at Barnum, a station outside of Thompson, the smoke had so increased as to render objects almost indistinguishable; farther down, at the lower stations, electric lights were lighted in the mills and the gloom continued to increase. Fourteen minutes before we reached the place where the train finally stopped it became absolutely dark, the lamps were lighted in the car but it was impossible to discern anything outside; and this condition lasted for just fourteen minutes, when we ran out of it into a dim smoky atmosphere through which the tops of the trees and immediate objects could be discerned. During all this time there was no sign of actual fire, nor could we even discern the reflection of fire upon the smoke on either side of the track. About a mile from Hinckley the train suddenly stopped, and at the same time the smoke lifted and the location of

Hinckley was visible; from it light smoke was curling up, but the sky was visible in patches. We then supposed that we had gotten out of the smoke. Just as we stopped a number of people came running through the underbush and woods on the left side of the track towards the train, crying and making indescribable noises; there were men, women and children, and the number seemed between twenty and thirty. As they got to the wire fence, fencing the right-of-way they tore themselves through the fence, the men tearing the women through, throwing the children across, and seemingly entirely demented and crazed by fear. Not having seen any fire, this condition of things was unintelligibie to most of the passengers. For myself, I stepped out upon the platform and down to the ground on the left side of the train, and while the sky was reasonably clear in front it was suffocatingly hot and the ground appeared to be very much heated. Just as I stepped back upon the platform I heard a roar as of a cyclone or tornado, and the trees upon the west side of the track were bent and twisted as though by the beginning of a cyclone which apparently came from the southwest. I stepped across to the other side of the train and looked towards the southwest, when a sudden blast of hot air struck the car, requiring the closing of the door. After it passed I stepped out again and just as I did so ascertained that the roar was caused, not by a cyclone of wind (although the wind was blowing very heavily), but by a burning cyclone, or mountain of bright flame which was rolling up from the Grindstone river directly upon the train. I stepped back and closed the door of the coach, and about that time the train commenced to move backward. It had only gone a short distance when a rush of flame struck it, breaking out the glass in the doors of the car and in the smoking-room, setting the latter on fire. I then stepped back in the coach through the smoking-room and found the aisles crowded with the passengers, numbers of whom were women and children. The train was gathering headway to the rear all this time, but in what seemed a very short time there was a rush of flame all over the train, when every window on both sides of the car burst out and the flame seemed to envelope the train top, bottom and side, setting the coach on fire on both sides, on top and on the roof. The passengers pulled down the rubber blinds in the chair car, but these only lasted a moment when another wave of flame swept through burning those up, and the flames swept through the car each side and through the windows. During this time the male passengers were passing wet handkerchiefs which were wet in the cooler, and the linen covers of the seats in the chair car which had been torn off were saturated with water and passed to the women and children to protect them. At one time the train gave a lurch and we supposed it was off the track, but it was evidently the force of the wind that had lifted the car and we continued to rush backwards. For a moment we passed out of the flame, and the smoke pouring in at the windows from the outside was sensibly cooler than the flame or air had been, and we supposed we had escaped, but in a moment later discovered that the train was so thoroughly on fire that it was impossible to put it out. In a short time, the duration of which I cannot give, the train stopped and the passengers in our coach (which was then on fire entirely for the first third and on fire underneath at the rear and all through the roof) got out upon the right of way on the west or right hand side of the train as it faced towards St. Paul. Here some one cried to go back into the train and not to leave it, and some of the female passengers attempted to do so but they were pulled back, as the train was then uninhabitable and was simply a roaring mass of flames. The group of people, consisting of eight or ten, in which I was, laid down on the right of way, keeping their faces close to the earth and crawled toward the fence which was distant fifty feet from the track.

It was suffocatingly hot, we were blinded by smoke and the rush of the hot air, and were covered by the cinders that were flying in all directions. We, however, succeeded in crawling through the right of way fence and getting to a patch of sand which was some twenty or thirty feet west of the fence. There again the sirocco-like hot air almost overwhelmed us, but we lay prone upon the ground, and by keeping our faces almost buried in the sand succeeded in escaping suffocation. One of the young men in the group said that there was water to the south of us, that he had seen the glint of it as the train stopped, and the colored porter, John Blair, who was heroically endeavoring to save the passengers of his coach, stood to the south of us and his back to the smoke and flame, sprinkling the prostrate women and children from a fire extinguisher. Some of the party crawled up on their hands and knees to the south, a distance of about two car-lengths, and then found by feeling that there was water, and upon returning the entire party scrambled, crawled and were pulled and pushed up to a little pond which afterwards turned out to be about sixty feet wide, and the women and children were rolled in it. Those who could not lie down crouched as low as they could get, and we remained there for a period that I cannot give but until the deadly heat and the flying cinders had somewhat lessened and the wind, still blowing with great violence and fully charged with smoke, was somewhat cooler. It was impossible to see objects at a distance of but a few feet on account of the smoke, and in addition all in our party were more or less blinded so as to make vision even more difficult, and it was only at intervals and with our backs to the wind that we could open our eyes at all; but having ascertained that the weight of the fire had passed over us, as we were undoubtedly in a clearing of a few acres in which there was no material to burn, we removed from the deeper water to a place where the water was only about six inches deep, and after lying there some time longer we again moved to where the ground was partially dry and finally moved out upon ground which was absolutely dry. By the light of the burning train, and particularly the tender, upon which the coal was all on fire and brightly blazing, I was enabled to get a glance at my watch and saw that it was just six o'clock; we had, therefore, been in the water or mud from about 4 or 4:10 p. m. until 6. We lay in groups upon the ground assisting each other to the best of our ability during the night and until 3 o'clock in the morning, when a party of rescuers from Duluth who had left their train three miles north of us came down with a physician and some lanterns. At four o'clock a relief party from Hinckley got through, and a little later hand-cars arrived bringing some milk, bread, water, and stimulants, which were sadly needed by the sufferers. At 5 o'clock the hand-cars were connected together with planks and the women and children and the most injured people placed upon them, and we started back for Hinckley, a distance of six miles, being over the road through which our train had backed. It is impossible to describe the appearance of the country. Before the fire it had been covered with a heavy growth of small trees, principally poplars, birch and tamarack; here and there among them were a few larger trees, and some of the older stumps were standing, but from Skunk Lake, where we had stopped, to the bridge at Hinckley and as far as could be seen on each side of the track the ground was swept as with a broom of fire; no vestige remained of the railroad fences, very little of the telegraph poles, a small portion of these latter being standing in some instances; and the herbage and foliage were absolutely swept from the ground. So great had been the heat that the ties were charred and burned, the rails in many places twisted so out of shape that the hand-cars had to be lifted around them, and the sides of the cuts presented a baked and calcined appearance; the bodies of deer and rabbits lay along the track, and when some two miles and a half from Hinckley we came across the first human bodies the full horror of the situation was apparent to us. Between the point where we stopped and the bridge at Hinckley on the road side inside the right of way and along the road were some twenty-two bodies, some in groups of three or four, others singly, all burned to a crisp and some of them partially consumed. It would be useless to attempt to describe these horrors; no words could give or paint the situation, and the effect upon the nerves of the survivors of our train when we came upon these scenes was a severe one, for there we beheld demonstrated what our fate would have been had it not been the heroic courage of our engineer and his fireman. Some slight idea of the volume of heat through which our train was run can be given when it is told that the coal on the tender was set on fire on the top and burned down through, and when it is further related that within a short time after our train stopped the entire train with the exception of the engine was reduced to smouldering coals; no vestige of any of the cars remaining except the iron-work, and the tender being filled with flaming coal which had not been consumed when we left there.

To James Root, the engineer, and his fireman Mc-Gowan, are due the credit of having saved the lives of the passengers on that train as well as the refugees from Hinckley who were taken aboard, on the occasion of our first stop. How they were enabled to do it is unintelligible to those who found existence almost insupportable inside of the cars, while those two men were in the very front of the flame which was pouring down upon them and only pro-

tected from it by the slighter structure of the cab.
The engineer was severely cut about the head by
the flying glass, and it is said fainted twice or three
times while running backwards and was replaced
upon his seat by the fireman.   The morning further
demonstrated his judgment in stopping the train
where he finally did, for there was no other point
within reach where there was sufficient clearing to
save the lives of the passengers, and the train itself
was entirely consumed within a short period of the
time that it stopped.   It could not have run backwards for three minutes longer without having
burned every person in it, for at the time of the
stoppage all of the cars were on fire both on the
outside and inside.   The porter of the chair-car,
John Blair, who stood in the rear of his group of
passengers and played upon them with the fire-
extinguisher, cannot be too highly praised.   The
conduct of the women and children in our car is
equally beyond praise.   They were cool, collected,
and obeyed orders absolutely.   I do not know of
any one, man, woman or child, in our car who
flinched from his duty, and while I presume nobody
expected that we would get out of the car alive or
that in case of getting out we would survive, each
acted with a self-possession that was simply wonderful.

No estimate of time can be given as to the duration of the actual horrors of the situation while

instant death was staring us in the face, but we stopped to take up the fugitives at either four or five minutes past four o'clock, we must have run back the five miles at a high rate of speed, and probably arrived at Skunk Lake at 4:10 or 4:15. From that time until a quarter before six to six o'clock none knew whether we would survive or not. The conductor of the train, Sullivan, did his duty until the last. A short time before the train stopped he passed through it from rear to front reassuring the passengers and doing his duty to the fullest and most complete extent. It is said that afterwards he became insane; no one realizing the horror of the situation and the fearful responsibility attaching to his position could wonder at it; the only wonder is that the survivors of this train have continued to retain their reason.

Of course there were incidents of different kinds connected with that two hours of horror that stand out sharply in the mind and reflection of each of the survivors. I presume that none of them are alike or that none saw the same occurrence, but speaking for myself I can only say that while I remember them, I find it impossible to sit down and relate them, for as the mind reaches back over the occurrence the horrors are again renewed and seem more impossible of contemplation, than they were while they actually occurred, and every nerve was strained to preserve judgment and reason while they existed, nor can I now understand how it was possible that we were saved.

OTHER EXPERIENCES.

Mrs. E. W. Sanders, of St. Paul, was a passenger on the south bound limited that was burned at Skunk Lake, and passed the horrible ordeal, with much fortitude.   She was accompanied on the train by seven children, consisting of her own family and some cousins of theirs and they all succeeded in escaping death from the flames.   When the train reached Skunk Lake, Mr. C. D. O'Brien assisted Mrs. Saunders in getting her little flock together in safety in the water, and once there did not abate his efforts in their behalf, wetting cloths and throwing water over them until the fire in its intensity had passed.   Mrs. Saunders appreciated Mr. O'Brien's efficient services to herself and her children at their time of need, and is loud in expression of gratitude and commendation.   They lay in the water for nearly six hours, when feeling the fire had passed they made their way to the dry ground and remained their until relief came in the morning when they were taken to Hinckley on the handcars, and from thence to her home in St. Paul.

It was an awful experience for anyone to endure,

DR. E. L. STEPHAN.

and for a lady of Mrs. Sanders temperament it was especially so, yet through it all she never once lost her presence or mind or self-control, and proved herself, as a woman can, equal to an emergency which makes the hearts of stronger brothers quail with fear. Aside from the fact that she caught a severe cold and suffered more or less from the nervous shock, Mrs. Saunders and her proteges are none the worse for their experiences, yet they all feel that their lives hung by the merest thread and are grateful to an omnipotent power for their deliverance.

Mr. John Craig, chief of the Hinckley Fire Department, whose heoric conduct in fighting the fire has often been spoken of and whose good judgment warned the people that the town must burn in time and to save themselves, tells his story as follows: "About 2 o'clock we called out the fire department and went to the west side of the town. We had 2,000 feet of hose. At that time we never dreamed that the town would burn. From the point where we were working we saw the fire start in the other side of town. They came after us to leave where we were and go and help those on the east side, so we started over. I telegraphed Rush City for more hose. When I came back up town I found everybody gone. I got my wife on the Eastern Minnesota train, but they got away before I could get my mother and sister to it, and we finally got into the gravel pit."

Dr. E. L. Stephen, of Hinckley, who was con-
spicuous both at the time of the fire and in the trying days that followed, says:" I was in my office
until it got so hot it wouldn't hold me. I then
went out and went through all the houses in the
south part of the town to see that no one was left
behind. The men were all out fighting fire and it
was the women and children that were left. I
carried a number of children to the train. I don't
know how many. I should think though at least
twenty. I went into my office the last thing to get
some articles I wanted, and when I opened the
door the fire was right upon me, and I closed the
door again and waited until the first gust had
passed, I then ran and got on to the Eastern
Minnesota train. I went to Duluth, but came
back on the first relief train and walked about fifteen miles through Sandstone to Hinckley. I
counted forty-seven bodies at Sandstone.

The majority of the corpses showed no sign of a
struggle. They seemed to die almost instantly, not
from smoke or from fire, but from one breath of
the heated atmosphere. I saw one man in particular who fell while running, and his legs were in
just the position of taking the next step with his
arms stretched out in front of him. I shall never
forget the scenes of that fiery holocaust. It was
terrible. I saw people leave their houses and fall,
and perish within twenty feet of their door-step,

Rev Father Lawler
Dr. Cowan
Coroner
Angus Hay

and the heat was so intense that I was obliged in
my trip through the houses to hold my breath
from one house until I got inside and could breath
the cooler air of the next one.,,

Rev. E. J. Lawler, more familarly known as
Father Lawler, had perhaps as close a call as was
experienced in the fire. When the fire broke out
Father Lawler accompanied by his housekeeper
and a Mr. Flynn and his wife ran to the river. The
women had a seal plush cloak which effectually
shielded them from the flames, and as often as
Father Lawler heard a groan from those around
him he would go to them and assist and throw
water over them. His housekeeper became overcome by the heat and sank, but he caught and
raised her and she soon revived. After a time he
was himself overcome and fainted, but the thought-
fulness of a little lad who happened to be near by,
and who held the reverend gentleman's head out of
the water until he was able to protect himself
again, saved him. Those who died in the river, perished not from the fire, but were drowned. Father
Lawler's eyes were terribly affected by the smoke
and burning cinders, and it was necessary to lead him
the next morning as he could see nothing. Mrs
Flynn was taken to Pine City and cared for by the
Judge of Probate.

Dr. Cowan, whose picture is given here in connection with that of Father Lawler was the

coroner of Pine County, and of course much of the
work of caring for the bodies of the dead fell to
his charge. A work which he took up and carried
on without fear or favor, and in which he exhibited a degree of executive ability, which assisted
greatly in straightening out the tangle which they
found things in after the fire had passed.

To the efforts of Mr. John Y. Breckenridge, the
Pine City druggist, perhaps as much credit is due
for the assistance rendered an afflicted people as to
those of any other one man. At the time of the
arrival of the news that Hinckley had burned his
was the only drug store available to furnish supplies to the wounded and he immediately set to
work to arrange such articles as might be needed
from his stock for the relief of the sufferers, and
with his equipment of lint, linseed oil, etc., went
to Hinckley with the first relief train. He came
back to Pine City with the first train that brought
out the sufferers, and from that time forward for
three days worked incessantly without rest or sleep
to alleviate the afflicted. He was elected secretary
of the Pine City Relief Committee, and acted in
that capacity as long as there was anything that
the committee could do. Throughout the entire
period that Pine City found herself responsible in so
great degree for the safety and comfort of the
refugees, John Y. Breckenridge was in the front
rank. He proved himself a man in every sense of

JOHN V. BRECKENRIDGE

the word, and a gentleman worthy of highest tributes of commendation at the hands of a beneficent public.

Mr. Frank G. Webber, of Pine City, had the most revolting and gruesome task that could be assigned to anyone, that of superintending the interment of the bodies. He says: "I was on the first relief train that went up from Pine City and took four men and 5,000 feet of lumber to bury the dead. We started in Monday morning with twenty-one men: we found ninety-six bodies at the cemetary ready for interment; they were all burned beyond recognition. We dug a trench sixty feet long, six feet wide and four feet deep, and in this trench these ninety-six unidentified bodies were buried. Sixty-five of these bodies were buried without even a box for a coffin, and the balance were furnished that dignity. I went back Tuesday morning with the same men and finished the work Wednesday, burying in all 233 bodies. In handling the bodies we made a stretcher with two poles, and the bodies were rolled onto the stretcher and from that into the trench, which was dug on an incline. During the time that burials were being made, the men who did the work were obliged to keep up their nerve and strength in viewing these horrible scenes by the use of stimulants, but Mr. Webber during the whole three days took nothing in the shape of stimulants or nourishment but a

little milk.   The total number of deaths caused by
the fire will probably never be known, and it is certain that numbers of them will never be identified.
Parties of lumbermen and hunting parties are still
finding the remains of some unfortunate fellow
who had been overtaken and perished, leaving not
even a trace of his identify, and scarcely a trace of
his existence. So far as is now known the total
number of lives lost by the fire in all quarters is
476. Of this number sixty-three died at Sandstone; twenty-two at Pokegama: eleven in the
State of Wisconsin; twenty-two Indians and the
balance in Hinckley and its immediate vicinity.

CHAPTER XIV.

He author has made no attempt at elegance of diction in editing and publishing the following anecdotes and experiences of the survivors of the fire, but has aimed to convey the impressions wrought upon the different minds as they were related by some of the sufferers, when questioned as to the actual facts of the calamity as they appeared to them. Mayor Webster of Hinckley says: "I gave up all hope of saving the town. I went through the house and spoke to my wife and told her the fire was beyond control, and that she must get ready to go to the gravel pit with me. I went to the barn and got the horses out, after a good deal of trouble on account of the smoke When I got back to the house I found that my wife had gone, thinking perhaps I was already on my way to the pit. I then went over to the pit but my wife was not there. The eastern Minnesota train was standing on the track, and I went through several cars, but did not find my wife among the refugees. As there were several cars it was impossible for me to get through I thought she must be in one of them. I felt quite easy about her. I accordingly looked to see what I might do for others. Going up town I found a team hitched to a wagon without a driver. I got two women and seven children and drove them over to the gravel pit where I staid myself until the awful ordeal was past. After it was over I again took up the search for my wife, although at first I labored under the impression that she had gone to Duluth on the Eastern Minnesota train, but I have not been able to find a single trace of her or anything that could serve to identify her. She must have become biwildered and perished in the heat." When Mr. Webster became convinced that his wife had been one of the unfortunates who had died in their own door-yard, the realization of the truth nearly destroyed his reason, and for a number of days he seemed like one dazed, not of this world, yet in it.

Another story that was characteristic though perhaps not as pathetic as the last was that of Joseph Tew, a drayman of the town of Hinckley.

He said: "I am a fireman, and fought fire until
half past three when it was apparent that everything was going I went home and got my wife
and six children on the Eastern Minnesota train.
The train pulled out leaving myself, my mother
and my oldest girl behind. I then drove with them
to the wagon bridge, and turning the team lose we
descended to the river. We had no sooner reached
the water when a perfect shower of cinders and
fire fell over us, and I found a couple of old coats
and put over the women. After staying in the
water about two hours and a half we left the
river and went down to the pit and then to the
Eastern Minnesota round-house. Those who went
north across the wagon bridge were all lost. Why,
man, I could show you the place where the next
morning men, women and children were piled up one
above the other just as thick as those rocks there,
pointing to a pile of building stone near by. "I
only had an apron that mother gave me over my
head."

Walter Scott in charge of Brennan Lumber Co's.
store says: "I got away on the Eastern Minnesota. Wind blew sixty miles an hour. Up until
3 o'clock no one thought there would be any
danger for the town. Conductor Powers of the
Emergency Train was the coolest man I ever saw
in my life. The way he kept his nerve was something wonderful. One of the heroes that perished

unnoticed and almost unknown was Paul Liske
the tailor at Hinckley. He saved the lives of two
young ladies by picking them up and carrying
them bodily to the Eastern Minnesota train. Not
being satisfied with that he went back for others
and perished in the flames, being overcome by the
heat before he was able to save himself. Some
idea can be had of the heat at some points at least,
from the fact that at Hinckley, the steel car wheels
of some of the freight cars were melted into the
rails they stood on so that they seemed like one
piece of iron. It is an established fact that 1,200
degrees of Farenheit is required in addition to a
blast to produce this result by artificial means.

The escape of Kate J. Barnum the thirteen year
daughter of Dr. E. E. Barnum of Pine City is perhaps one of the most interesting episodes of the
horrible affair. She had been visiting at Hinckley
and had intended to return to Pine City on the
day of the fire. The friends with whom she staid
all went to the Eastern Minnesota train and she
went with them. She was not satisfied however
to go to Duluth, but thought of the "limited"
which was due at the other depot at 4:05, and it
occurred to her, if she could get on board that
train she could reach home and set the minds of
her parents at rest, as to her safety and where-
abouts. She decided to make the attempt and in
spite of protests she started for the other depot,

KATE J. BARNUM.

fifteen hundred feet away all alone, and with the
one idea in view of reaching that Depot and waiting for the other train. She reached the depot and
seeing the mill and lumber yards burning became
alarmed and went back to the Eastern Minnesota
train intending to remain with her friends and
make her escape. But the desire to get home was
still strong and a second time she left the one to
make the other train. A second time she reached
the other depot. This time she found the depot on
fire and also the bridge across the river. She then
realized the train could not possibly get through
and that her only hope of life lay in again reaching
the Eastern Minnesota train. Again she set out;
how this slip of a girl endured tortures and exposure that made the strongest men quake and
even fall is little less than a miracle. On her way
back the last time, she would run as far as she
could and then lie down on the ground and after
catching her breath would again run on and repeat the operation. The train was finally reached
and boarded, and another ray of sunshine saved to
a happy household. All through this terrible experience Kate had been entirely alone and as she
said herself, she did not seem to be at all afraid,
and it never occurred to her that she needed anyone to take care of her until she had reached the
Emergency Train the last time, when she seemed
to realize the peril through which she had passed

and wished for some one to take care of her. She found her protector in the person of Presiding Elder Shannon of Duluth, whom she knew, and to whose Duluth home she was taken and cared for until she could return to her parents at Pine City. Imagine if you can the feelings of a father who knew that such a daughter as this had been exposed to the flames and so far as he knew, had perished in a holocaust of this sort, and who was compelled by the call of duty to minister to the wants of others who had suffered from this same cause, for twelve long hours without any word of his daughter in any way and you will understand one reason that Dr- E. E. Barnum of Pine City has to remember that horrible day. Too much credit cannot be given Dr. Barnum of Pine City for his loyal devotion and heroic self-sacrifice to the work of alleviating the pains of the suffering and wounded survivors. His time and professional services were given freely gratuitously day and night, without rest or sleep for a period of seventy-two hours. Everything he could do was done freely and willingly even to the free use of his bank account in purchase of medicines and hospital supplies. He is in truth one of nature's noblemen, we are glad to be able to give a likeness of him with this volume. The face is one that shows a man of unswerving integrity, earnest, sincere in all his dealings, conscientious, true to his highest ideal of right.

DR. R. R. BARNUM OF PINE CITY

A man who commands not only the respect but the
love of the entire community in which he lives and
one, whom, the humblest of his patients can point
to, proud to be able to call such a man their
"friend." At the time the news was first brought
to Pine City he was the only physician in the town
and upon him devolved the responsibility of caring
for the wounded sufferers. He accompanied the
detachment of citizens of Pine City on the first expedition to Hinckley. Their train was composed
of eight hand-cars joined together with rough pine
boards making a continuous train on which were
transported the injured people that were picked up
along the road. When the remains of a burned
bridge was reached the train was disconnected,
and the sufferers were either carried accross on the
ten inch iron girders or down through the stream
and up on the track again at the other side. Dr.
Barnum's train of hand-cars was the first to
reach the Skunk Lake survivors from the south after the fire. They carrried the cars around the
bridge and went on from there to the point where
Root's train had been saved, picking up thirty-
three dead bodies, and two men who had lived
through it along the track. Soon after reaching
the spot they made their way to Engineer Root
and he was given a drink of milk from the hand
of Atty Roberts, who singularly enough had been
instrumental in times past of having Root arrest-

ed and fined on account of some trouble in stopping the "Limited" at Pine City. The fireman McGowan was still throwing water and caring for his injured chief. An overcoat was put upon him and he was sent to Pine City. The responsibility of overseeing and directing the care of the wounded fell upon Dr. Barnum, although Dr. Cowan and Dr. Stephan of Hinckley, Dr. Harris of North Branch and two physicians of Rush City, besides two members of Dr. Barnum's family did much of the routine work. He had charge of the improvised hospitals at Pine City and for the first ten days never relaxed his vigilant attendance upon, nor his duties to them although he was greatly relieved by the removal of eighteen of those whose injuries were of the most serious nature to St. Paul and Minneapolis hospitals.—John Hogan of Hinckley is a cripple. On account of some affectation of tha hip he is unable to wa'k a single step and was of course absolutely helpless when the fire broke out, he says;- "I had been watching the fire and had made up my mind in case worst came to worst that the gravel pit would be the place for me. My brother had been out fighting fire and came in with his team and I called to him to take me to the gravel pit, he came, lifted me out of my chair and carrying me sat me into the wagon and took me over to the pit. Once arrived there it looked so terrible I asked him to put me on the Eastern

Minnesota train, that we might get out of the horrible place entirely. He did so and then went back to the house after my mother, she refused to leave without my invalid chair, so he put that on and they brought it with them and so it was saved. My brother did not get on the train and for two days in Duluth we could get no news of him in any way, but we finally found him, and you had better believe a happier meeting never took place."

Mrs. Alex Cameron, of Hinckley, in speaking of the fire says: "My husband is a millwright. On the day of the fire we were out fishing at Grindstone Lake. About 4 o'clock the sky was overshadowed and everything became as dark as mid-night. We lighted the lamps in the camp, but soon we found that the fire was upon us and we ran for the boats and put out into the lake drifting with the waves. The wind was something terrific and the waves were running so high that we expected every instant to be swamped, but decided we would rather drown than burn. When we got across the Lake we found an Indian camp and found some potatoes which we cooked and which served to allay the pangs of hunger. After staying in camp over Sunday, Monday morning we started to walk to Hinckley where we arrived after a tramp of about ten miles over the burned ground."

Molly McNeil says: "About 2 o'clock I tried to induce my folks to get away on south-bound limited that left at that time, but they laughed at me. I then packed my trunk and tried to get it to the depot myself. A man came along and told me to drop the trunk and save myself. So I started out on the north road toward the river. I ran right straight across the bridge, being bewildered, I suppose, and when I came to my senses the river was half a mile away. Mrs. McNamara and her family were with me up to this time, and someone spoke of Root's train which they said would be along soon. I had forgotten all about the train, and told Mrs. McNamara we had better hurry to meet it. I ran on but she did not follow and that is the last I saw of her. I reached the train and we soon commenced backing up until finally Skunk Lake was reached. I jumped from the bridge, my only thought being to find water enough to drown myself. My clothes were all afire and I rolled over in the mud and behind an old barrel that was there. While I was there I noticed a large snake coiled up beside me, but that didn't trouble me, I had something else to think of just then. I was in the water about two hours and got to Pine City about 8 o'clock the next morning. I must have been about a mile and a half from Hinckley when I met the train.

Miss Mary McNeil, an older sister of Mollie's

had a different yet not less exciting and terrible experience than was endured by Mollie herself. At the time of the outbreak of the fire she was with her mother who was eighty years of age, and together they started for the river. Mary says: "Mother told me to go back and look for Mollie, and I turned and started back, but could not endure the heat so we started for the river again, before we got there a wave of heat swept over us that was terrible; it seemed to strangle me and I fell; I said "Mother we will have to die right here," but as it was only a little ways further we made another effort, and succeeded in reaching the river. We got to the water and only had an apron to throw over our heads. We stayed in the water about three hours. While we were there we saw several people die around us." It is a singular fact that the old lady in her eigtieth year should have been able to undergo the terrible ordeal, endure its excruciating pain and survive it in the end, while strong men placed in similar circumstances perished beside her.

Probably the most miraculous escape of the fire was that of Al. Fraser, of Hinckley, and his family, and it is more than probable that he of all the survivors endured the greatest heat and lived to tell the story. He had a wife and three children, and managed to get one of the children on the Eastern Minnesota train, and then got out to help his wife and the other two, but the train was so crowded that they were not able to get on board, and the train pulled out without them. They then went back into the town and he found a team, and loading his family on to the wagon drove out of town on the north road in the direction that proved to be so fatal to so many of the towns people. They went directly across the wagon bridge, and soon the heat became so intense that their wagon caught fire and burned furiously. They all got down onto the ground fully expecting that their last hour had come, and that they were doomed to perish there in the flames. In speaking of it afterwards, Mr. Fraser, said: "After we had turned the first team loose, I noticed something coming toward me through the smoke which proved to be another team of horses and wagon which had been abandoned by their owners. I caught the team and loading the wife and little ones into the wagon drove on. I found four barrels and a trunk on the wagon, and after driving a little way I found that the barrels were full of water. Just think of it, four barrels of water at a time when above all things else water was to be most desired. I put my children right into the barrels, and broke open the trunk, and wetting the clothes I found there I put them round my wife. About that time two Norwegians came along and crawled into two of the barrels that we had used most of the water

out of, and so escaped with their lives at least.
One other gentleman was also saved by the water
which put in its appearance so fortunately. Mr.
Frazer was within a short distance of the dry swale,
in which the one hundred and twenty people
who went out on this north road lost their lives, at
the time the terrible heat had reached them, and
he says of it: "When that wave struck them one
wail of anguish went up from the whole people as
one man, and in less than a minute after everything was still except for the roar of the wind and
the crackling of the flames   It all came so quickly,
an instant and all was over. There did not seem
to be much suffering. There could not have been
much. There was not time. A moment after that
first intense wave had passed not one of those
hundred and twenty people were conscious, and I
do not believe they were alive. The next morning
when they were found the bodies did not seem to
be badly distorted as if there had been a struggle
for life, but they were found lying on their faces in
the sand or else on their backs with their hands
clasped over their mouths, showing their last
thought must have been one of protection from the
fiery breath."

CHAPTER XV.

MORE EXPERIENCES.

IMILAR though the stories of the survivors may be they differ in detail. Of course all have the same general characteristics and recite an experience excruciating and terrible. Their similiarity is especially noticeable in the towns where numbers chose a similar avenue of escape, but in the outlying districts over which the fire had passed, the escape of the settlers was attended by perils often more appalling and always more varied than that of the towns men.

It is the purpose of this chapter to give an idea of escape of some of those who were in the country districts when the fire reached them. The escape of the family of J. Erickson, a resident of Sandstone, is remarkable. On the day of the fire Mr.

Erickson, with two sons and one daughter were at
Sandstone Junction where he owned a small saw-
mill and quite a piece of ground, and were engaged
in harvesting the small crop of potatoes the
ground had produced in the drought of the
summer. His wife and one daughter were at the
postoffice at Sandstone, and one daughter of the
family was teaching school at Partridge. At the
first approach of the flames Mr. Erickson and the
boys went to fighting fire about the mill, finding
they could not save it they went to the potato
patch, and as that soon proved too hot for safety,
not to say comfort, they started for a small lake
about a quarter of a mile distant. It soon
became so dark that they became confused,
and in some way the old gentleman became separated from the children. They could hear each other
call, although the smoke was dense, sight was impossible a short distance away. The children got
into the wagon and made their way to the lake in
this way. The old gentleman became completely
turned around, got off the road and was going
directly from the lake when he heard the voice of one
of his boys calling him; he answered and guided
by the sound found the boy and made his way
to the water where he found the other children
with the team. As the first burst of the fire swept
over them the horses became frightened and got
away from the boy who was holding them and got

burned.   After the fire had passed they walked to
Sandstone, three and a half miles and found that,   .
as Mr. Erickson tersely expressed it.   "All gone to
h—l."   After wandering around awhile they made
their way to the river and found the wife and
other daughter.   At the first approach of the fire
they thought it was a cyclone and went to the
cellar.   They discovered their mistake, however,
and after doing so had only five minutes to reach
the river before the storm burst over them in all its
fury.   The girl got out the money belonging to
Uncle Sam and saved that, but left quite an amount
of her own money in the house, which was already
burning, and as they were leaving the steps of the
store the roof of the whole structure fell in so that
they were none too soon.   The daughter at Partridge also made her escape, so that here was an
exception to the rule, a family whose ranks had
not been decimated by the fire.   The case of
Thomas J. Henderson, deserves more than passing
notice as being one of the saddest and most
pathetic incidents of the whole affair.   Mr. Henderson is a. logger who lives at Pine City, but who
had gone with his two sons, aged fourteen and sixteen respectively, to a point about five miles north
of Hinckley where they were engaged in opening a
new road through the woods for the St. Paul &
Duluth R. R.   In speaking of the fire Mr. Henderson, said: "I was working with my two boys

about a mile west of the track when the fire approached.   We had noticed things looked a little threatening, but anticipated no danger until the fire was nearly upon us when we started for Mr. Greenfield's house about a quarter of a mile east of the track. When we reached there we found the family going to the cellar of the house and we went in with them. We had been there but a short time when it became apparent that none of us would escape if we staid there long, so we crawled out and ran for a potato patch close by. Our clothes were burning as we left the cellar, and I had a hard fight to put out the blaze. After I did so, the boys one after the other became overcome with the heat and died right there before my eyes. Mr. Henderson escaped though his right hand was terribly burned. After the fire had subsided he made his way to Pine City where he met his wife, who seeing him come alone without her boys realized the truth before a word was spoken, and with a wail of "Oh, My God! My boys are gone," burst into a paroxysm of tears and moans. "Yes, they are gone," answered the bewildered father, and for days after that the mere mention of the fire would throw him into convulsions.

Mr. M. E. Greenfield, at whose home Mr. Henderson and his boys sought refuge fared even worse than Mr. Henderson. In speaking of the affair he said: "I had defended myself against fires on the earth.   I had no idea that fire was to come down upon me from heaven, but that was what it did. Soon after we entered the cellar a shower of living fire began falling all around us, thicker than any hail storm you ever saw, and carring the coals and embers from the burning of the lumber yards at Hinckley.   In the cellar with me were my wife and six children, my hired man, John Parrish, and Mr. Henderson, a neighbor, with his two little boys. When the house began burning over our heads we determined to stay in the cellar as long as we could, for we thought every instant that torrents of rain would surely fall, for the sound we heard was exactly like heavy thunder, and kept coming nearer. When the floor began to fall in, and the dining table crashed through upon us, we saw that to remain there was sure death, and we opened the outside cellar door, and tried to all get out. My wife and all of my children got out. John Parrish, I think, must have fallen back into the cellar way after helping out two of the children. Mr. Henderson also got out, and I can not say whether his two boys perished in the cellar or somewhere in the clearing. After all were in the potatoe patch in the clearing, one of the children, the oldest girl, ran back into the burning house, and I found her bones among the ashes of our ruined home. In the fields I tore the clothing off from all of the children to keep them from catching fite, and watched over them and my wife, going from one to another when I heard them cry out—for it was impossible to see anything—until I thought that all of them were dead; when I lay down, expecting nothing less than that in a few moments I, like them, should be dead. I was soon aroused by a cry from my ten-year-old boy, Charlie, who is here with me. He wanted me to help him put out the fire in his mother's clothing. That call for help saved all our lives. I had been directly in the path of the hot air blowing from the burning house, and when I went to him I escaped from it, and found the air quite endurable, for the worst heat from the fires at Hinckley had passed. I found my wife still alive, and we succeeded in putting out the fire in her clothes, although she was terribly burned. My little boy kept his presence of mind through it all. He tells me now that he kept from burning up by rolling in the dirt to put out the flames which started in his clothes. I do not know how I escaped with so little harm, for during all the time I did not think once of saving myself."

Mr. Greenfield was found in a very despondent mood, and expressed the opinion that it would have been better if all had perished together, for he said he had not a cent in the world, and would not know what to do to provide for himself or his family, now pitifully small. He was greatly en-

couraged when told of the generosity of all people
in contributing to the relief fund, and seemed
greatly rejoiced over the bare possibility that there
might be even a little help for him. He says that
the fiery cyclone tore up the roots of some of the
largest trees on his farm and carried them long
distances through the air. Mr. Greenfield's hired
man John Parrish, of whom he speaks, must have
gotten out of the cellar with the others as his body
was found six weeks after about three-quarters of
a mile from the Greenfield homestead. In his effort
to escape he had followed an ox away from the
house depending on the animal's instinct to lead
him to a place of safety. When he was found dead
by the side of the ox his hand was still clinched
with a firm grip on the ox's tail, which means he had
undoubtedly used to keep from being separated
from what he hoped was a means of escape.

The name of Mrs. A. G. Crocker, of Finlayson
deserves a place with those of the heroes of the
fire. Mrs. Crocker is a slender, delicate looking
woman, but many a man might envy her heroic
spirit. After fighting the fire demon all day
Saturday and discovering that her house was
about the only one left in the place, she gathered
there all the neighbors whom she could find, thinking as she said. "I could give them something to
eat, and if the necessity arose, we could all take
refuge in the little pond near my house."

About 5 o'clock a fearful roaring was heard and the cyclone of fire rushed upon them. They all ran for the pond, wrapping the children in wet blankets and throwing water over each other. There they staid until near midnight, throwing themselves down in the water as the waves of fire would pass over them.

By this time the women and children were so chilled and stiff, they decided to leave the pond and fight the fire from the house which was again in great danger of burning. The children were left on the shore of the pond, and the women and Mr. Crocker fought fire until daylight, and all day Sunday they all alternated between the fire and pond, seeking relief from fire in the pond.

Sunday night Mrs. Crocker made her way to the railroad and flagged the relief train as it went down to Hinckley. She was told to get her friends together and they would all be brought to Duluth on the return of the train.

"Then," said Mrs. Crocker in telling of her escape, "ensued another night of fighting for our lives. By this time we had used up all our provisions and when the rescuers picked us up Sunday night or Monday morning, whichever it was, we were completely exhausted and could not have held out another hour." Nevertheless Mrs. Crocker immediately went to work, doing all she could for those less fortunate than she.

Mrs. Crocker returned to Finlayson Wednesday, taking with her a supply of provisions for the sufferers there. As her house is standing, she said there was a great deal she could do sheltering and feeding the homeless there.

The fate of the Best family who lived about two miles south east of Hinckley is one of the most heartrending incidents of the whole affair. Out of a family of thirteen, John Best Jr., and his wife and child are the only remaining representatives, and upon this one man, John Best Jr., devolved the task of giving a decent burial to his father, mother, four brothers, two sisters, one neice and a friend who happened to be stopping with the family at the time.

Express Messenger Vandersluis of the Eastern Minnesota train that was ditched and came so near being consumed between Hinckley and Poke-gama on the day of the fire tells his story as follows:

"When we got to Hinckley everything was smoke. It had been that way for two weeks, so we didn't take any particular notice of it. We left Hinckley at 2:30 Saturday afternoon. When we got one mile out everything was as dark as night and one mass of flames. Our train consisted of an engine and baggage car and coach. When we got five or six miles out of Hinckley we noticed that the ties were burning under our train. We

went through this for about five miles, expecting
every minute to go through bridges, as we felt
them weakening under the weight of our train.
All of a sudden the engine jumped the track and
turned over on its side, the coach following, but
keeping upright. There were but two passengers
aboard, and these, together with Conductor Ed.
Parr, Engineer Will Voge, Fireman Joe Lacher and
three brakemen and myself, made up the list of all
on board.

"About 5 o'clock Saturday evening the conductor and myself walked over to Pokegama, two
miles away, over the burned ties, passing three
charred bodies on the way, with their faces buried
in the sand. When we arrived at Pokegama Creek
we discovered that the span bridge had been
burned and also the entire village of Pokegama.
All the villagers that were saved were in Pokegama
creek, panic stricken. We returned to the coach,
and shortly after the people in the creek walked
on to our coach, in all about twent-five men.
women and children. We stayed there until Sunday morning at 5 o'clock. It was a terrible night.
The experience I shall never forget. We tore up
our shirts and everything in the way of linen and
soaked them with water, and kept them over the
faces of the two passengers and the people from
Pokegama. They were suffering terribly, being
choked and blinded. The conductor, engineer,

firemen and myself left for Hinckley, leaving the
brakemen and others in the coach asleep or partially so. We found nothing at Hinckley, except the
Great Northern four-stall roundhouse and water
tank and coal shed. We went into the water tank
and found some good water of which we drank
freely. We also found several loaves of bread,
which we broke and ate. We then went into the
roundhouse and found some bread and crackers,
which we sent back to the sufferers in the coach,
and this party was afterward rescued by a relief
crew from Pine City.

"At least 100 cars of wheat and other mer-
chandise was burned in the Hinckley yards. We
walked around to where the St. Paul and Duluth
depot formerly stood, and took a train carrying
sufferers to Pine City. An abundant supply of
food and clothes had been sent from Pine City,
and the sufferers were being taken care of as fast as
possible. We saw the dead lying all around. We
stayed in Hinckley about twenty minutes. Everything was filled with smoke, and we could not see
a block away. I do not think that the reports are
at all exaggerated."

The following clipping from a Duluth paper is
directly in point as it gives· "Honor to whom
honor is due." Presiding Elder W. A. Shannon,
who was on the Eastern Minnesota passenger
train—the first to return from Hinckley Saturday

THE LAST OF SEVEN.

night—makes the following mention of a courageous act that has until now escaped recognition:

"As one of those who took the perilous ride from Hinckley to Duluth on the Eastern Minnesota train in ths midst of the fiery furnace of Saturday last, I wish to add my testimony to the courage and bravery of the trainmen. It took nerve to stand still with flames leaping toward and around them on the wings of a tornado—as these men did—till 500 people should get on board. Conductor Powers and the crew of the freight train which joined us in the mad rush for life, indeed every man connected with the service is deserving of highest praise."

"I wish especially to refer to O. L. Beach, the brakeman of the passenger who took his stand on the tender of the freight engine— which was backing up and without head light —and never flinched through all that perilous ride of sixty miles through smoke and flame.

"Such devotion to duty on the part of these men under such trying circumstances is worthy of public recognition. No one who took that awful ride will ever forget the men who brought us through in safety to Duluth.

The following account of the coming of the great fire is related by Mrs. James Garnness of Finlayson, whose farm stood on high ground overlooking Hinckley, Sandstone and the surrounding

country. About the middle of the day, which was
an intensely hot one, the air grew so heated that she
could not hold her hand up over her head for any
length of time. It was like plunging it into an
over heated oven. Then the air gew so hot lower
down it was almost impossible to breath. Looking in the direction of Hinckley they saw flames as
if darting from the sky in "tongues," and
"sheets," and watched the terrible spectacle grow
more and more awful. The town of Sandstone
then became enveloped in the same kind of flame,
while Hinckley was lost sight of in the dense
smoke. The flames spread rapidly, and though at
first they could not believe it possible the fire would
come as far as they were, they very soon saw there
was almost instant danger. The first appearance
there was a ball of flame which fell from the air
and lighted beside the gate of the front yard, burning itself out without spreading in the least like a
gasoline flame. Then these became more frequent
and they saw that all the country was to be enveloped in the rushing whirl of fire. The very air
seemed to burst into flame; the heavens rained
fire, and the clouds above so close to earth opened
and shut, making the alternate light and darkness
almost blinding. The family all went to some
ploughed rising ground back of the house, carrying with them large cans of water and blankets.
They had to move very quickiy for the heat grew

so intense, and the flaming air came nearer and
nearer, and the darkness enveloped all things. The
whole family crawled under the blankets, which
one of them from time to time would wet from the
large milk cans of water beside them, and this
they did by thrusting out their hands quickly and
upsetting first one and then another, as the
blankets grew hot almost to bursting into flames,
while their houses and all that belonged to them
burned. They lay under the blankets for hours,
and when the worst had passed, spent the night on
the ground longing for day. When it came the
sight can better be imagined than described.

There are many strange freaks related as to this
extraordinary fire, and one of them occurred at
this place. Two farm machines, one a harrow and
one a reaper stood on a field not far apart. The
harrow was scarcely scorched though made of
wood, but the other was completely burned, even
the iron and steel parts melted into a shapeless
mass by the intense heat.

CHAPTER XVI.

ANOTHER STORY—SOME PERTINENT FACTS.

ENTERPRISE, has always been and still is the watchword of Hinckley, and in the race, Mr. Angus Hay, editor of Hinckley Enterprise is always to be found in the front rank. It affords a pleasure to me to be able to give those who may peruse these pages the story of one, who took such a prominent and important part in the events which we have essayed to chronicle in this little volume. The reader may be assured that the tale is honestly and modestly told, and certain it is, no hero ever faced a dangerous task with more fortitude than was displayed by Angus Hay and his companion Carl Veenhoneen, in their perilous trip over a smoking and burning track, when they carried the news of Hinckley destruction to Pine City and the outside world. Mr. Hay writes as follows:-

"The experience of one who has passed through the Hinckley fire! The truth would seem like the mildest fancies of crazy imagination; no pen can portray its terrible reality; no tongue can even tell the bare truth of the awful ordeal. At the noon hour word was given that the villagers west of the St. Paul & Duluth tracks were being hard pressed by flames which threatened their homes. Chief Craig of the fire department ordered his men out, and volunteers followed the firemen to assist in saving the property. The fight was a noble one; the west side of the village and the Brennan Lumber Company's mill plant were in great danger; the hose was too short to reach the spot where the fire was the greatest. The chief telegraphed to Rush City for hose. The alarm was growing greater, and every man and boy in the village who could leave his home was carrying water to quench the flames. At short intervals the wind was so hot it almost blistered one's skin. The men worked like beavers to keep the flames from crossing to the main part of the village east of the track, and every one was confident the fight was won, but the fire which started from the Mission Creek fire came stealthily along like a tiger. The wind blew a hurricane; strong men were hard pressed oftentimes to move against it. The south-bound train on the Duluth arrived at 2 o'clock—two hours late—and many of the women and children went south to places of safety. From this hour on the fire had control, though it met a worthy foe in the gallant little band who fought it for supremacy. Women became alarmed, but their fears were quieted by those who were none the less in fear, but who had cool heads. The southmost house on Main street was Nels Anderson's; on saving this home depended the safety of the village. Teams hauling water, were dashing along the street; women were afraid, and children were crying; men's faces were a study—bleached with smoke and driven sand and blanched with fear for the safety of their homes and their families.

Chief Craig came dashing down the street on his horse and cried, "We can't save the town; it's burning at the south end; run to the gravel pit; don't lose a moment, but fly!" Then commenced a hurrying and a scurrying for safety such as I believe few, if any, in this place ever took part in or saw or ever will see again. I was four blocks from my office when Anderson's house caught fire. I ran as quickly as I could to the office and when James Willard, my faithful typo, and I ran through the office to the rear door large coals were falling in the yard. We intended saving several articles in the print shop, but soon gave the idea up when we saw distressed women and children trying to reach a place of safety. Picking up the "Enterprise" files and a "fat" subscription book we went out to help those who needed assistance. Some woman with three children was tottering along the sidewalk. I picked up her baby and carried it until I saw a man driving with a horse and buggy toward the Eastern depot. I put the little one into the rig and went back to help the mother. The Eastern train had left the depot then and the mother and children were put in the gravel pit. I went down the street again to the corner of the Morrison hotel, but could not endure the heat around the corner. It drove me back, and I ran for the gravel pit. I saw a woman crossing the Duluth tracks at the round house. I believe now it was Mrs. Blanchard. Her body was found there. She seemed to strike her foot against the rail and stumbling, fell. Two people were on the streets.

Two women were praying in front of the city hall; one was on the driveway, the other on the grass beside her. With unintentional disrespect I stopped the prayer meeting and started the ladies for the pit. Water was better than prayers just at that moment, and I'm glad the women are safe. Seventy people—men, women and children—huddled together in that muddy pond with but three feet of water. It is a block and a half long and half a block wide. Houses on the east and south and the depot on the west were all burning. The wind blew direct from the south, and a continual shower of coals and sparks fell on us. Then began an ordeal of fire lasting about twenty minutes through which I believe few could stand to pass again. It was terrible in the extreme. It was necessary to keep throwing water on the women, and it devolved upon very few men, to do it. Such a time as that one wishes he had as many arms as an octupus; the Lord knows they could have been used to good advantage. The roar of the storm was so great it was impossible to make one's self heard two feet away. But the wind would carry the almost inaudible mutterings of a prayer along to leeward, and the hearers, I think, uttered a silent "amen." We got out of the water in two hours and a half after entering it, and the hot winds too soon dried our clothing. About seven o'clock those who had saved themselves in the river began arriving at the pit. They were the worst used up crowd I have ever seen. Most of the women had to be supported by strong arms and the children were carried. Then the first volunteer search party of the great fire went down to the river, where a young man said he saw dead bodies in the river. The party pulled out Mrs. Martin Martinson and her three children, and helped others out of the water who were unable to move. Most of them would have died in a short time if left there very much longer.

At half-past eight the survivors of the holocaust who had remained in town straggled down to the

Eastern Minnesota railroad round-house, the only building saved in the village. From the round-house a good view could be had of the ruins, and though our eyes were sore and swollen from the smoke, heat and sand, and though we gazed on the ruins of home and business, the scene presented was grandly fascinating. It reminded one of the great panorama of the "Destruction of Pompeii." The streets looked like some climax in a grand drama, the golden glow from the burning buildings lighting up the scene in a manner strangely grand. After a couple of hours rest in the round-house, seven of us organized for a trip to Pine City to get relief. We took a hand-car and started. Our trip was necessarily slow, as the rails were warped in places and we were afraid the culverts were all burned out. It was my first experience as a pilot on the road, and I confess I know little of the track, but the work was to be done, and it was. At Mission Creek we met the work train putting in new culverts and repairing the track. After considerable talk, we persuaded them to return to Pine City. "Hinckley is burned" spread with lightning-like rapidity through the village, and its inhabitants were not slow in coming to the succor of their unfortunate neighbors. The north-bound limited, which was waiting there for orders, was loaded with provisions and men anxious to assist in the relief work. Arriving at Hinckley, food was given to the hungry and the sufferers were made as comfortable as possible and taken to Pine City. The work crew, with four hand-cars loaded with relief men, started for Skunk Lake, where the south-bound St. Paul & Duluth limited was burned. We arrived there about three o'clock in the morning and found the belated passengers camped beside the slough. We loaded passengers bound for St. Paul on the hand-cars and began the return to Hinckley about daylight. Along the track was strew some thirty bodies who had succumbed to the fire and heat. At one point a woman lay, face downward, her arms outstretched, and under each arm lay two little children. She bared her body to the heat in the hopes that her little ones might be saved. At another point the paternal love of a father was shown in the same way for his eight-year-old boy. Coming back to Hinckley, we were told by Allen Fraser, the man who made the greatest fight and won in the Hinckley fire, that more than a hundred dead bodies lay in the marsh where he had saved his wife and little ones and two men. The report was too true. It was a gruesome sight, indeed, to see at first at daybreak a field of two acres covered with one hundred and thirty burned bodies. No battle-field ever could present a sight so terrible when death in its most horrible form mowed down its victims. In most cases there was little suffering before

HINCKLEY'S FIRE CHIEF JOHN T. CRAIG.

death. The victims, apparently, were suffocated with smoke before the cruel flames lashed their bodies. Sunday afternoon organized relief corps assumed charge of the work, and from this on the gruesome task of burying the dead and allieviating the suffering of the burned was carried on.

Any one item in any one instance could be woven into columns of truth—startling, and, to one who was so fortunate as to have never had the experience, seemingly unreal.

But Hinckly will rise again. Its business men are of that true blue stamp that can never be discouraged. Its people are sincere in their undertakings, and have confidence, and justly, too, in the future of the village. Though the fire made the loss enormous as to property and inestimable as to life, it placed it twenty years ahead as a farming country. When the legislature meets it will probably be called upon to place monuments in memory of those who fell at Hinckley, Sandstone and Pokegama.

When we again hear the songs of the birds in the summer, and the golden grain is being gathered in autumn from the fertile soil around Hinckley, the tale of the great Hinckley fire will be still being told.

I would be ungrateful indeed were I to end this feeble sketch without, as one of 1,500 people, extending my most sincere thanks to all the people of the country for the generosity, kindness and assistance given these people when "a friend in need was a friend indeed." Words are inadequate to express the feeling which wells up within me when I would thank the people for their kindness.

ANGUS HAY.

Rev. P. Knudson, the Presbyterian minister at Hinckley, proved himself worthy of bearing the title of a shepherd of his flock, for no shepherd was ever more solicituous for the welfare of those under his charge than was Mr. Kundson and his estimable wife in this hour of trial. In speaking of the affair, he said that over two hundred of those who were burned might have been saved had they heeded advice and kept away from the river. "The fact is," he went on, "they lost their reason and stampeded like a lot of frightened cattle headlong to destruction. Some tried to escape by teams, and they were found dead in a heap afterwards. I never saw a sadder sight. The horrors of a battlefield are nothing in comparison. None of us expected to be alive when the fire waves passed over us, and those who did escape were alone and helpless on the charred desert without anything to eat or drink. Few had any clothes. I got six burned watermelons, and they were devoured by the people in the twinkling of an eye. My wife milked one of the cows which escaped in the pit, and that kept the children's bodies and souls together. The Eastern Minnesota's water-tank, the only structure left above ground, was afterwards discovered, and proved our salvation. Providence alone saved that for us. We were all too blind to see each other."

The greatest sorrow caused at Hinckley was occasioned by the horrible death of Thomas G. Dunn, telegraph operator at the St. Paul & Duluth station. Mr. Dunn was a universal favorite with the boys of the St. Paul & Duluth. He was the greatest hero of all the railroad men. He waited at the key in the telegraph office for orders for the limited train due in five minutes. But no orders came, no train came, and the depot was burning over the brave boy's head. Friends tried to persuade him to leave his key, but he remained until every passenger had left the depot. No one else could do it. Other depots were closed. No one could give orders; no train could leave. His grave is hallowed by the salt tears of the entire community as well as by his fellow workers on the line of the St. Paul & Duluth. His name will always be remembered as worthy of the highest praise, and an elaborate monument will be erected by his sorrowing friends to mark the spot where he lies.

Another very sad case is the death of Orlando Rowley. He was on the limited that burned at Skunk Lake, and when the fire had passed his body was found about three hundred yards from the point where the train had stopped in a little trench which runs from the shallow water to a swamp near the lake, which he had undoubtedly entered and followed, thinking by this means to reach the lake and thus find deeper water and safety. Mr. Rowley was the general passenger and freight agent of the Duluth & Winnipeg road, and was quite well known in both of the Twin Cities as well as Duluth.

The list of heroes of this great fire will never be enrolled save in that list where every man's deeds are recorded.

There was the engineer of the "limited," who picked out the only green spot for miles and bore two hundred souls to safety through the terrible ordeal, standing erect in the roasting heat, which only iron fibres could endure.

There was the little hero, a West Duluth boy of fourteen, who dragged two smaller children along the weary miles from the wreck of the train to salvation, where rescuers found them.

There was the young lover who carried his sick betrothed for a mile through the flames on his back to a place of safety, while the heat was so intense that others walking beside him, and with no burden, lay down to die.

There was the man who, after fighting the fire for two hours, took up a crippled brother and bore him in safety to the relief train.

There were telegraph operators who, by quick decision and quicker action, saved hundreds of lives.

There was the daughter who stayed beside the bedside of her mother, who being in the pangs of maternity, could not be moved, and who was not to be dragged away from sharing her mother's death until forcibly pulled from the already burning house.

There was gruff and good-natured Bull Henly, the Hinckley sectionman, who stood in the road and turned the steps of the flying people towards the gravel pit.

There was little Freda Johnson, of Sandstone, who saved the lives of her father and mother and that of her little brother by inducing them to go to the river instead of into the cellar as they had intended.

There were the dozens of men whose positions in death, as it instantaneously seized them, showed they were hastening at all speed into the very face of flames to the rescue of loved ones.

It were useless to attempt to enumerate them all. Heroes were on all sides, indeed it required heroic attributes to enable anyone to endure such scenes and still retain their presence of mind enough to assist those who were weaker and less fortunate than themselves.

A general survey of the district after the fire had passed revealed a great many incidents which were interesting and at the same time hard to account for.

Among the many unidentified dead was a large man frightfully burned. Underneath him was a fragment of one of the pockets of his pants. In this charred receptacle were three silver dollars melted together, also a number of coins of smaller denominations. Close alongside him was a set of loading tools for a shot gun, but no gun was found in the vicinity. Scarcely two feet away from the body was a flask full of powder which had not exploded, nor did it seem in the least affected by the fiery ordeal, although part of the brass work of the flask was melted into a common mass with the copper sides.

At Sandstone on the damaged bridge of the Eastern railway the north and south approaches were reduced to cinders while the middle span was intact, and on this part of the structure was found a large dog which had evidently run onto the bridge and was hemmed in by the fires at both ends. He remained upon his perch on the bridge for three days, and when a bridge man finally climbed to where he was he immediately attacked the man rather savagely, and it was thought he had gone mad and that they would be obliged to shoot him. This did not prove to be the case, however, and he was lowered with a rope and taken to Duluth, and henceforth will bear a name which it would seem even he might remember, that of Sandstone.

Near Skunk Lake is another and deeper body of water, and into this life-saving pond some fifteen settlers crept, followed not only by their domestic animals, but by two deer, two timber wolves and a big black bear besides smaller wild animals.

Close by the river at Hinckley on the south side is the remnants of a kitchen garden. A large number of cabbages are there and they are thoroughly cooked, as well as some potatoes, carrots and onions. All the trees, big and little in the enclosure, are totally destroyed, yet a light picket fence is almost unhurt.

An unknown Swedish woman and child were found in the Hinckley swamp close to town. The woman was lying on the charred leaves of a Swedish Bible. Late Saturday evening some charred leaves of what appears to be part of the same book floated down from the clouds and landed in Duluth on First street near the Kitchi Gammi club house.

One woman, when she saw the flames approaching, and seeing no means of escape, thought to lessen her danger by throwing the contents of a barrel over herself. There was not a great deal of it, and she thought it was water, but it proved to be kerosene! Imagine the condition of that woman when the flames surrounded her.

Another instance connected with the fire that will prove interesting: Engineer C. P. Fadden and Fireman N. Reider, of the St. Paul & Duluth railway, were bringing crippled Engine 19 on one side, light, from Duluth to St. Paul, and had reached Hinckley before the fire. The dispatcher was just sending him orders for continuance when the fire reached the wires south of Hinckley and they went down. This tied him up at Hinckley with his engine, and when the flames struck the town, without going through the formality of asking permission, he ran his engine over the Eastern Minnesota tracks and backed down near their round-house, which was protected slightly by an open patch and a grove of green trees, and was the only building left standing in the town. The engine was slightly scorched and lagging burned, but her crew stayed with her and brought her out in good shape.

Engineer Fadden is next to Root in standing rights, having been on the road since 1872, and when asked for a description of the conflagration at its height, flames and smoke being all around and over him, replied "he had been in hell, and saw everything there was to be seen except Satan himself."

Another instance which illustrates the capriciousness of the fire was the case of a farmer living a short distance from the St. Paul & Duluth track, which he reached and was following in an attempt to escape until he became bewildered and exhausted by the heat and smoke, and concluded he would have to give up and that his time had come. Blinded and suffocated, suffering intensely from the heat, he ran into the woods at the side of the track and there fell unconscious. When sensibility returned he found himself in the center of a little plot of ground not over twelve feet square, which had been spared by the fire. Hearing a hand-car pass a short time after, he made his way with difficulty to the track and received aid from the relief band. He told the men his story and showed them the spot where he had lain, and everything on all sides of this one spot had burned to a crisp.

A team of horses were driven into a clearing and saved, yet the neck-yoke of the wagon was burned from the tongue.

Numberless incidents of this kind could be cited, which seem almost incredible to one who has not actually seen them. For instance. a young sapling was found growing and in good condition not six feet from a tree thirty inches in diameter, which had not only been burned up, but the very earth at its roots had been cousumed.

A window holding at the same time both a sash and screen was found after the fire, one lying on top of the other, with the glass of the sash so melted over the wire of the screen that both seemed as one.

In the cellar of one house was found the remains of what was once a watch and chain. As it fell the chain hung out almost straight, and had been melted into a solid bar. The watch lay at an angle, the stem downward. The case had melted and collected in a lump where the stem had been and the works had been transformed into a shapeless mass attached to the other.

Foreman Jim Bean, of the Brennan Lumber company, who was lost, had left his watch hanging in his vest in the mill. A little heap of blackened metal was recognized as Jim Bean's watch by a little fragment of a thin, twisted chain which escaped the action of the fire to make it certain that its owner had gone to his death.

Perhaps more marvelous was the failure to burn of the claim shanty of Frank Baumcher, just below Mission Creek on the east side of the Duluth tracks. Loosely put together and covered with ragged tarred building paper, a more inviting object never was exposed to fire. Green timber went up in in smoke. yet it was overlooked, perhaps as being to valueless to cut any figure in the total of destruction.

Trees were hollowed out and burned into all sorts of grotesque shapes. Telegraph poles were burned off in the center, leaving the stump below and the top with its cross-arm dangling from the wires above.

Where there was not enough above the surface to satisfy the appetite of the fire it ate its way down into the depths along the roots of the trees.

Rather an odd circumstance was that experienced by J. T. Clark and Tom Campbell, of Hinckley, who on the day of the fire were fishing at Lake Eleven, and who were counted as dead. They had no idea of the extent of the disaster, and, as they succeeded in escaping themselves, did not attempt to return for several days. Finally a search party was sent our for them, carrying spades and expecting to bury them where they were found; and it proved a surprise party indeed for all concerned, as the searchers were met by those whom they sought on their way home and still very mnch alive. It is needless to say that the burial was dispensed with in this particular case. Sandstone can boast of an attraction which even Barnum hasn't got, in the shape of a one-eyed pig that somehow or other got out of his pen and into the river. His companion was literally roasted alive, but "Paddy," as he is called, escaped, and he is now a privileged character and the pet of the town. He has only one eye left, but, as one of Sandstone's citizens says, "He's no fool of a pig, and he can lick any dog in the town."

The druggist at Hinckley, speaking of the holocaust, says: "I filled three barrels with water and left them standing on the platform of my well. After the fire the only thing that was left of those barrels was the bottoms, heads and hoops. They were barrels that had been water-soaked, and still they burned."

That the Indians of the section shared the fate of their pale-face brethren is vouched for by the following clipping from a Duluth paper:

"POKEGAMA, Minn., Sept. 7.—A courier brings a report that the bodies of twenty-three Chippewa Indians, bucks, squaws and pappooses, lie upon the baked sands between here and Opstead, a small settlement on the eastern shore of Lake Mille Lacs. They are scattered over ten miles of country, and will in all probability prove food for buzzards and wolves, as the country where they died is too far from civilization for burial ceremonies.

"The Indians left their reservation two months ago and built a hunting lodge along one of the forks of Shadridge creek. Chief Wacouta was the "big chief" of the party, and he perished with his followers. The first body found by the courier was that of an infant barely a year old. Then came those of two squaws and five children. They had evidently turned west when the flames swept the forest. A ride of a mile brought him to a pile of ashes, which marked the site of the hunting camp.

There was one tepee, the shriveled raw hide thongs marking the place where it stood. Around it were the ruins of a half dozen birchwood bark shanties, and protruding from the ashes were the fused barrels of rifles and shot-guns. Then for five miles the pathway was lined with charred bodies.

Pokegama Lodge, Knights of Pythias, which is located at Pine City, deserves honorable mention for the part it played during the great calamity. As has already been stated, the ground floor of the hall belonging to this lodge was turned into a kitchen and dining room for the use of the sufferers. There were nine members of this lodge that were in the fire, three of whom were burned to death. The lodge cared for the these members, as K. P.'s are always cared for, and in addition quite a sum of money was raised by the lodge, not only for their afflicted brothers, but also for the outside sufferers. Dr. E. E. Barnum, Dr. E. L. Stephan, Dr. Cowan and John Y. Breckenridge, who have been before mentioned as prominent in relief work, were all members of this lodge, and not only these, but all members of the order did all that was in their power for the sufferers. Pokegama Lodge has exemplified the teachings of the order, and words of praise are heard on all sides from the people at Pine City toward the order of Knights of Pythias in general and Pokegama Lodge in particular.

CHAPTER XVII.

THE perusal of the foregoing pages cannot fail to give the reader an impression of the calamity of which it treats, sad in the extreme; but at the same time to those of a more sanguine temperment, comes a feeling akin to pride, in the realization of the fact, that they are citizens of a commonwealth, which in truth is a government by the people and for the people, and that in spite of the fact that by this dire calamity whole counties had been laid waste and hundreds had been made homeless and penniless, their sufferings had been relieved in every manner possible by the munificence of their fellow citizens, as soon as the combined forces of lightning and steam could carry relief to them. It brings a realization of " the fatherhood of God and the brotherhood of man." No one who passed through the fiery furnace and escaped, could fail to appreciate the words of one of the fire heroes, Engineer Wm. Best, who in speaking of the calamity said: " I'm not much of a church-man. We railroad men seldom are, but there's one thing, my friend, I tell you, God almighty was good to us that day."

And for those whom we call less fortunate, to those that have passed beyond, is it for us to say that God in his Infinite Goodness, was not merciful to them, too ? They have simply reached the border that must come soon or late, and its passage was made so quickly they scarcely realized their fate. A moment and all was over, a breath of that hot gas and they were unconscious, another and the soul had passed. This is without doubt the manner of death of the majority of the victims although invariably the bodies were afterward so burned that recognition was impossible. The only gratifying feature of the whole horrible affair has been the manner in which the whole people responded to the call for assistance. One touch of sympathy makes the whole world kin. Never was a truism more aptly spoken and never was its truth more fully exemplified than in the States of Minnesota and Wisconsin in the few days immediately following the fire. Almost as one man, high and low, rich and poor, capitalists, laborers, professional men and merchants, ladies who were society leaders and those whose paths lay in the humbler walks of life, showed the best sides of their natures and contributed freely to the fund, which was to be used to aid the sufferers. The work was noble, unselfish, quiet and unostentatious, because the pall fell upon all alike, and the people mourned with the mourners, and suffered with the sufferers, because their hearts and minds were tonched and they felt that the least they could do for their brothers in this, their time of affliction was to give from their bountiful store that which was needed most and they could spare best. Another train of thought which might be followed to some length in connection with the fire, is its origin and the cause which led up to it, from a scientific stand-point. Much has already been written on this subject, and whether its origin was electrical, or was generated through spontaneous combustion, or caught in the old-fashioned way it is not in the province of the writer to decide; neither will he consider the question as to whether the fire generated the wind or the wind begot the fire, but is satisfied to say that nothing so terrible in its effects, or in its appearance has ever come upon any people. Even the description Bulver gives of the destruction of Pompeii is not too much to apply to the destructive elements of this holocaust in the vicinity of Hinckley and Sandstone. The loss to the section in dollars and cents will never be known and is certainly very difficult to even estimate, but it is estimated that $12,000,000 will cover the total loss to the lumber interests and citizens in the section covered by this great fire. This is over $2,000,000 larger than the estimated loss in the Johnstown disaster of 1889, and the loss is certainly more wide-spread and effects a class of peo-

ple more dependent upon what little they had in
the world, in that they were farmers, and in many
cases the product of years of toil and cultivation, were wiped out and they were left totally dependent, without even an axe to begin a new life
with. The loss of life in this case was about one-
fifth of the loss in the Johnstown flood and the
contributions for the relief are about one thirtieth
of the amount received to alleviate the sufferers of
the Pensylvania calamity.

Inasmuch as thisvolume has portrayed the dark
side of one of the blackest chapters in the history
of the States of Minnesota and Wisconsin. it is
only fair that a few pages should be given to the
brighter side, or the prevailing conditions in the
country and a few facts which might prove interesting to prospective residents of the garden spots of
the world.

In the rush to the prairies beyond; the great and
varied inducements Minnesota offers to homeseekers, investors and promotors of industrial en-
terprises have been strangely overlooked. The im-
pelling motive that led the early settlers to seek
the prairies of the far west and the Pacific shores
left no room for scrutiny of the fertile areas they
were passing over. Besides the extensive tracts of
rich alluvial lands along the many rivers and
around the innumerable lakes and the countless
mill streams, affording perpetual water.power for
manufacturing purposes, there are in addition im-

mense areas of mixed timber and prairie lands dotted over with never failing springs, lakes and running streams of pure clear water to entice the stock-raiser, wool-grower, gardener and all, who wish to engage in any line of diversified farming. With a healthful climate all the year round, every variety of soil for all the products of garden and field, with excellent transportation facilities and convenient markets, there are all the factors that contribute to the health, comfort and prosperity of the industrious settler.

There are millions of acres in the state now to be had at from $2 to $5 per acre, on eighty acres of which any industrious man could make his family comfortable and independent, after enduring for a short time the toil and privation incident to the making of a home on unimproved land. In a few years at the rate at which desirable land is being occupied the present splendid openings will be no longer within the reach of the incoming home-seeker. With its delightful climate, health, excellent water, cereal crops, grasses, wealth of minerals, stock raising capabilities, unsurpassed timber, an industrious peaceable people, this great grain, stock and dairy country, Northern Minnesota, offers unparelleled attractions to all classes of immigrants.

Many people in the east have little or no idea of the true conditions of life and the accompaniments of civilization to be found in the west. The prevalent conception of eastern people is of Indians in native garb and reckless cowboys with an absence of the comforts of civilization and law and order of settled communities. They are surprised to be told that civilization in many respects is in a more advanced stage in the west than in the east. Many small towns of Minnesota can boast of electric lights, electric railways, telephones, telegraphs, water-works, libraries and a fine class of public, commercial and resident buildings, unequalled in towns of similar size in the eastern states. The western man quickly hears of what is new in science, religion, literature or business, as he is vigorous, intelligent and quick to move; he has adapted and is using the electric force to light and heat his house and propel his railways, the power of steam to plow his fields and thresh his grain before these improvements are generally employed in similar ways in the east. Owing to the rapid growth of settlement his live newspapers, churches, schools, societies and the desirable social conditions are soon established.

One of the first things thought of by a man who contemplates removing his family to a new country is the facilities for educating his children. No doubt many have been deterred from settling in the west by a groundless fear that the newly settled district would not have the educational

advantages, religious privileges and pleasant sur-
roundings that they would desire and conse-
quently have turned aside to less desirable regions
farther south. As far as Minnesota is concerned a
few facts will dissipate this fear. This state has a
permanent school fund $11,508,800, This rich
endownment is more than double that of any
other state in the Union, Kansas and Texas, ex-
cepted, and very much larger than either of these
alone. No state in the Union has a more compre-
hensive school system, embracing common schools
where the rudiments of all branches of education
are taught, high grade schools, normal schools for
the education of teachers, an agricultural college
and experiment station; a University and Medical
Colleges for professional training, and the deaf,
dumb and blind are taught whatever modern skill
or science can impart. These institutions have
ample pecuniary aid and are under charge of
teachers who will compare favorably with those
of any other state. The permanent fund of the
State University is considerably over one million
dollars, and in number of students ranks third
among the universities of the United States. The
annual revenue for the support of the schools of
the state is $3,700,000. The above list does not
include denominational universities and colleges of
which there are a large number. There is probably no state in the Union that pays more for the

HINCKLEY AS IT NOW APPEARS.

support of all classes of educational institutions and none pays it more cheerfully than Minnesota. No state makes a more generous provision for its public schools or has a more complete and effective system; and among the attractions of this state and the inducements it holds out to intending immigrants none are more worthy of attention than these facilities for popular and religious education.

There are over five million acres of free government lands in the various counties of Northern Minnesota still unoccupied, and the Northern Pacific, St. Paul & Duluth and Great Northern R. R. Companies offer over two million acres of land for sale at prices ranging chiefly from $2 to $6 per acre and on easy terms. To the rich and varied resources of the state combined with its healthful climate is due its rapid advancement in population and wealth. There have been 1,328,336 acres of government lands taken up in the past three years and the remaining five million acres may be expected to be appropriated in the near future.

Three important river systems have their source in Northern Minnesota, the Mississippi, the Red River of the North and the St. Louis and other streams flowing into Lake Superior. This position of Minnesota at the head of the waters, so to speak of the continent, is typical of her commercial and industrial situation.

Northern Minnesota consists of diversified timber and prairie lands interspersed with innumerable lakes, streams, and natural meadows. Many charming locations can be had by the shores of the sylvan lakes and on the banks of the clear running streams. All the grains, grasses, vegetables and small fruits of temperate latitudes grow in profusion, and the convenient markets of St. Paul, Minneapolis, Duluth and Superior, and many prosperous towns throughout the state afford ready sale for the products of the forest, farm and garden. To those who wish to engage in general farming, stock-raising, wool-growing, dairying, gardening, poultry-raising, bee-keeping or the raising of small fruits no more attractive or suitable region can be found than Northern Minnesota. The woods abound in game and the lakes contain the finest varieties of fresh water food-fish, comprising black and rock bass, lake trout, white fish, muskallonge, pickerel, pike, perch, catfish, and wall-eye pike. The climate of the state is healthful and invigorating. The summers and autumns are nowhere more delightful. The dry pure air mitigates the summer's heat and modifies the winter's cold. The climate has for years been remarkable for its beneficial effects on consumptives, more particularly the pine forests regions of the north. The numerous lake resorts offer

every summer multitudes of visitors who are in
quest of health, recreation and enjoyment.

The recent extensive forest fires have accomplished for the settler what would otherwise
require years of unremitting toil. Over large areas
of fine agricultural country have the fallen timber
and underbush been completely cleared from the
surface, leaving comparatively little to be done by
the settler to prepare the ground for agricultural
operations. This is eminently true of extensive
areas along the line of the Northern Pacific and
St. Paul and Duluth Railroads.

PINE COUNTY.

This is the county in which the effects of the
great forest fires were most severe. It occupies an
especially advantageous position being nearly
midway between St. Paul and Duluth at the head
of the great lakes. The county contains 1,400
square miles of land and has twenty-six lakes
within its borders. A large number of streams
flowing into the St. Croix and Kettle River, one of
its largest tributaries, drain all parts of the county.
It is not as its name implies a pine country for
two-thirds of its surface is covered with a fine
growth of maple, oak, ash, elm, hickory, birch,
linden, aspen and other hardwoods. The surface
is gently undulating and rolling and hilly adjacent
to some of the larger rivers. Lumbering up to the

present time has been the leading industry, but since the fine agricultural resources of the country are becoming better known rapid progress in settlement may be looked for. A fine quality of sandstone is found along the Kettle River, and the quarrying and shipment of stone gives employment to large numbers of men. In most of the county there is a fertile black soil about one foot in depth, underlaid with a reddish gray subsoil of clay. Wheat, oats, potatoes, garden vegetables, small fruits, etc., yield bountiful returns. There are 122,340 acres of free government land awaiting settlement, and there is much cheap railroad land belonging to the St. Paul & Duluth and Northern Pacific Railroads. Two railroad lines traverse the county and the advantageous location of this region to markets renders it an inviting one to prospective homeseekers. The farmer, stockraiser, gardner, horticulturist, dairyman, or those who wish to raise small fruits or poultry will find in this county inducements unsurpassed by any other portion of the United States, and to the industrious a comfortable living, and early competence is nowhere more assured.

The present population of the county is 6,000 and the principal towns are Pine City, Hinckley, Sandstone, Willow River, Finlayson, Rutledge, Sturgeon Lake, Partridge and Kerrick.

The "Lake Park Region" largely comprised

in counties of Becker, Otter Tail, Douglas and
Wadena is the most picturesque and romantic
portion of the state. It consists of beautiful
undulating prairies interspersed with groves,
lakes and fringes of forest trees, the timbered
areas becoming more frequent and densely covered
as the higher portions of the region are reached.
Very much of it is an intermingling of woodland and prairie, and in considerable areas there
is little undergrowth, and large black oaks
with widely spreading tops stand far enough
apart for the thick growth of grass to thrive beneath them, giving the locality the appearance of
a well kept park. This feature gives it the name
of "Park Region." In the wooded district there
are occasional marshes partially covered with
growths of cedar, tamarack, cranberries or wild
rice. No more perfect pleasure resorts are to be
found in any part of the world than are afforded
by the beautiful lakes of this region, embowered
by groves and possessing the park-like features
already described. This was the veritable paradise of the Indian, and it is scarcely less attractive
to the civilized men of to-day. It is the ideal
country for a home. Its waters and forests are
full of life. The soil will produce liberally everything that the farmer wishes to raise and reward
his industry with a plentiful harvest. Wheat,
oats, rye, barley, peas, flint-corn, timothy, the

clovers, vegetables and small fruits yield bountiful returns. Nowhere is the natural herbage more abundant, botanists have enumerated about 150 species and varieties of native grasses among which the most prevalent are blue-joint, northern red top, timothy, white clover and meadow oat grass.

The soil varies from black sandy loam to clay and sand in places. The cutting and hauling of cordwood, railroad ties, poles, pile timber, staves and wood fibre and pulp for paper manufacture furnish employment to large numbers of men and teams during the winter season. Settlers of limited means can in this way do much to support themselves and famiiies while establishing a home, and those on timbered lands in the neighborhood of saw mills and railroads can clear their farms free of cost. · Many are also employed in the extensive iron mines and lumber camps of the northern counties.

In the " Park Region " all conditions are favorable for the raising of cattle, horses and sheep. The grasses are nutritious, the pastures are green all summer, hay is abundant, the numerous lakes, ponds and streams afford pure water to every farm, and the dry crisp cold of the winter is conducive to health in the animals. They do not run down during the winter months as they do in wet and changeable climates. Of almost every industry pursued in Minnesota an equally favorable account can be rendered by the inhabitants of the "Park Region." Even corn, which is supposed to flourish best in warmer latitudes can be cultivated successfully here.

There are several million acres of government lands yet open for homesteading free under the United States land laws in the Lake Park Region and in Aitkin County. The Northern Pacific Railroad Company also offers for sale over one million acres of land in these districts at prices ranging chiefly from $2 to $5 per acre and on five years time if desired.

Among the towns of this region may be mentioned Brainerd, Detroit, Wadena, Perham, Fergus Falls, Lake Park, Park Rapids, Motley, Verndale and Aitkin.

AITKIN COUNTY.

This is one of the newer agricultural counties of the state, and little more than one-hundredth part of the more than one million acres included in the county is under cultivation. The soil consists of a sandy loam with a clay subsoil, and the surface was formerly mostly timber with the exception of some fine meadow land in various portions of the county. The recent forest fires swept over more than a third of the county leaving many cleared areas inviting to the settler. The forest portions

consists of belts or patches of pines and other coni-
fers, alternating with areas of deciduous trees;
maples, the ashes, ironwood, oak, basswood, elm,
and poplar, the pine prevailing in the northern
part. Considerable sugar and syrup is made in
the districts where the sugar maple abounds.
Cherries, wild plums, strawberries, currants, goose-
berries, blueberries, grapes and cranberries are
abundant. There are numerous beautiful lakes
well stocked with whitefish, bass, trout, pickerel,
pike, sunfish and other varieties. Half of the
magnificent sheet of water known as Mille Lacs is
in this county. This lake has an area of about 204
square miles and is deep with clear, pure water and
gravelly bottom. Its waters are so clear that objects fifteen feet below the surface may be plainly
seen. Its banks are high and firm except at the
south end where Rum River issues from it. There
is hardly a lake in the world of similar size that
affords so many beautifully residence sites on its
shores or better facilities for boating and fishing. The county is well watered by numerous
tributaries of the Mississippi, and is crossed east
and west near its central portion by the Northern
Pacific R. R. which own 95,000 acres of land within
its boundaries. There are also 96,000 acres of
free government land awaiting occupancy. Con-
sidering its advantages this county offers superior
inducements to settlers. The principal towns are

Aitkin, McGregor and Kimberley.   Other villages and postoffices are Attica, Libby, Hickory, Malmo, Nichols, Portage and Wealtchood.

Northern Wisconsin is greatly diversified in surface consisting of heavily timbered pine uplands, lakes, rivers and tamarack swamps. As Lake Superior is approached, the country becomes more rugged, the shores of the lake being picturesque and beautiful. No better trout streams are found on the continent than these which enter Lake Superior from the Wisconsin shores. In Washburn, Sawyer and Bayfield counties are numerous lakes abounding in nearly all varieties of fresh water fish. Wild game, including deer, moose, partridge, grouse, bear and occasional cariboo are found in the woods and geese and ducks are very plentiful on the lakes in their season. Like Northern Minnesota, Northern Wisconsin is the paradise of the hunter, trapper and fisherman, and its soil and timber has many attractions for the farmer and woodsman.

In the counties mentioned above there yet remain 144,287, acres of government lands open for settlement. There are numerous prosperous cities and towns in this region, among which are Superior, Ashland, Bayfield, Hayward, Shell Lake and Barronett. Lumbering operations are very extensively carried on and the farming communities are rapidly extending.

For particulars regarding lands and other data of interest to a person contemplating investment or removal to the Northwest, application can be made to Mr. Wm. H. Phipps, Land Commissioner of the Northern Pacific Railroad Company, St. Paul, Minn., and full information concerning the country will be furnished them.

LIST OF PERSONS WHO ARE KNOWN TO BE DEAD

John G. Anderson
Mrs. John G Anderson,
Charles Anderson,
Emily Anderson,
Mrs. Cora Abbey,
Albert Abbey,
Floyd Abbey,
Lloyd Abbey
John Burke.
Burke's father.
James Beon,
John Best.
Mrs. Eva Best·
George Best.
Fred Best.
William Best.
Bertha Best.
Victor Best.
Nels Eck.
Andrew Edstrom.
Edstrom's mother.
Mrs. Erickson's friend.

Miss. Annie Truttman of
Diamond Bluffs Wis.,
visiting with Bests.
William Costegan.
Mrs. Effie Costigan,
Effie Costigan,
Irma Costigan.
Myrtle Costigan,
Jennie Costigan,
Billy Costigan,
Hazel the baby.
David Cain,
Mrs. David Cain.
Mike Currie,
Mrs. MIke Currie.
Tom Corbett.
Louis Chambers,
Pat Fitzgerald.
Mrs. D. Donohue;
Mary Donohue.
Katie Donohue.
Esther Donohue.

Mrs. Pat. Fitzgerald.
John Fitzgerald, 14.
Mary Fitzgerald, 13.
Patsy Fitzgerald, 12.
Mrs. Nelson Frick.
David Frick, 10.
Fred Frick, 8.
John Frick, 6.
Richard Frick, 4.
Mrs. W. Grissinger.
Collie Grissinger, 10.
Mable Grissinger, 8.
Nathan Hopkins.
Mrs. N. Hopkins.
Mother Hopkins;
Sister Hopkins.
Louis Nelson.
Peter Johnson, 35.
Mrs. Annie Johnson, 31.
Annie Johnson, 12
Tom J. Jones, 40.
Alfred Johnson, 29,
James Kelly, 43.
Thomas J. Lowell.
Mrs. Thomas J. Lowell.
Esther Lowell.
Chester Lowell.
Mrs. Lind, Skunk Lake.
Four children of Mrs. Lind.
Mrs. Betsy Nelson.
William Nelson,
Otto Olson.
Three children.

William Ginder.
Mrs. Wm. Ginder,
Willie Ginder, 9.
Jennie Ginder, 9,
Winnie Ginder, 8.
James Gonizar.
Emma Dolvan, 24.
Belle O'Brien, 20.
Annie Wallace, 28.
Henry Hanson.
Mrs. Clara Hansen.
Ed. Hanson, 32.
Mrs, Ed. Hanson, 29.
Annie Hanson, 18.
Hilda Hanson, 6.
Edwin Hanson, 4.
Jessie Hanson, 8.
Mrs. John E. Hanson.
John McDonald.
John J. McDonald.
Mrs. Jas. McNamara.
John McNamara.
James McNamara.
Michael McNamara.
Mike Murphy.
H. W. Mathiason.
Mrs. M, Mathiason.
Baby Mathiason.
Ida Mathiason, 9.
Emma Mathiason, 7.
Hilda Mathiason, 5.
Martinson's Child.
Mary Nelson.

Four Children.

Peter Peterson.

William Penoyer.

John Rogers, 39.

Mrs. John Rogers, 36.
Mary Rogers, 4.
Maud Rogers, 2.
Baby Rogers, 7 days
Chris. Rustin.
Mrs. Chris. Rustin.
Three children.
Paul Schlanow 26.
Mrs. Karine Stjerpka, 29.
Mrs. Noble Sherman.
Romazo Sherman.
Leslie Sherman.
Johnnie Sherman.
Flora Sherman.
Fred Sherman.
Mrs. Fred Sherman.
William Sherman.
Bina Sherman.
George Sherman.
Earl Sherman.
Ralph Sherman.
Old Tom, 56.
Anton Weigel.
Mrs. Anton Weigel.
Girl 4 years.
Mrs. Thomas Westby, 34.
Sophie Westby, 8.
Samuel Westby, 3.
Louis Wold, 34.
Alfred Wold, 12.

Gustave Newstrom.

Mrs. G. Newstrom.

Two Children.

Maggie Nyberg

Dennis Riley.
Mrs. Dennis Riley.
Tom Riley.
Jamie Riley.
L. Reynolds.
Mrs. L. Reynolds.
Three children.
W. Richetson, 58.
Mrs. W. Richeton, 58.
John Robinson, 44,
Mrs. John Robinson.
Three children.
Otto Rowley.
John Ross,
Mrs. H. Paulson.
Joseph Stromberg.
Mrs. Joseph Stromberg.
Charles Stromberg, 21.
Oscar Stromberg, 13.
Albert Stromberg, 11.
Mary Stromberg, 9.
Augusta Stromberg, 6.
———— Stromberg, 22.
Mrs. Geo. Winretter, 24.
Thomas Westby, 38.
Tom Westby, 10.
Ginder Westby, 5.
Baby Westby, 1.
Mrs. Louis Wold, 30.
Ida Wold. 10.

Christ. Wold, 6.
Grand father, Wold 62.
Mrs. John Westman, 32.
Mrs. Westland, 25.
Her sister and child.

Child 1.
John Westman, 36.
Child Westman, 2.
Sophie Waski, 29.
Baby Waski, 1.

POKEGAMA DEAD.

Fred Molander.
Two children.
Mrs. Chas. Anderson.
Oscar Olson.
Mrs. Olson, St. Paul.
Thomas Raymond
Three children
James Barnes.

Mrs. Fred Molander.
Charles Anderson.
Three childreen.
Nora Olson.
Charles Olson.
Mrs. Raymond
Erick Larson.
Mr. Whitney.

David Goodell.

PINE CITY.

Sandy Henderson, 13.

John Henderson. 12

ACTUALLY IDENTIFIED.

Axel Hanson,
Tom Dunn, opr.
Jerry Crowley,

Bill Nesbitt,
Dennis Riley,
Mrs. Martinson and her

five children who were drowned.

WISCONSIN'S DEAD.

Alex Erickson.
————Williams.
Maggie Bargron, 25.
Mrs. Tawney, 26.
Walter Graft, 18 months.

Theophile Bedard.
Frank Bargron, 30.
Isaac Tawney, 47.
Elisha Tawney, 6.
Willie Tawney, 13.

Jessie Tawney. 4.